A GOOD BAD IDEA NOVEL

ARIELLA ZOELLE

Copyright © 2020 Ariella Zoelle

www.ariellazoelle.com

Ariella Zoelle originally published Bet on Love as A.F. Zoelle.

All rights reserved.

This is a work of fiction. Names, characters, places, and incidents are products of the author's imagination or used fictitiously. Any resemblance to actual persons, living or dead, is purely coincidental. All products and brand names are registered trademarks of their respective holders/companies.

This book or any portion thereof may not be reproduced or used in any manner whatsoever without the express written permission of the publisher except for the use of brief quotations in a book review.

Cover Design by Adrijus of Rocking Book Covers

Editing by Pam of Undivided Editing

Proofreading by Sandra of One Love Editing

Layout by Ariella Zoelle of Sarayashi Publishing

ISBN: 978-1-7324473-9-4

WELCOME TO SUNNYSIDE!

Immerse yourself in the world of interconnected series set in the fictional town of Sunnyside

Full of cute sweetness and sexy fun, every story ends with a satisfying HEA and no cliffhangers. Since all of the following series are set in the same town, you can expect to see cameos of your favorite characters! The books are funny, steamy, and can be read in any order.

Good Bad Idea: Romances featuring bad ideas that lead to true love. It starts with Rhys expecting to wake up hungover after his bachelor party—not married to his best man. His biggest surprise is falling in love with his new husband.

Suite Dreams: Couples fall in love at Luxurian Suites Hotels all over the world, starting with Jude and Rigby. Their meet-cute in an airport on a snowy day leads to a hotel room with only one bed and a happily ever after.

Dedication

For the fun of trying something new.

Chapter 1

Lucien St. Amour

IN LESS THAN FORTY-EIGHT HOURS, my best friend was getting married. I should have been excited for Rhys, but I wasn't. How could I be when Olivia was all wrong for him and I was losing him forever?

She had insisted on a daytime bachelor party so the groomsmen wouldn't be hungover at the rehearsal the next morning. While partying with our friends had been fun, it had been a struggle to get through it, knowing Rhys would commit himself to a loveless marriage soon.

Once evening came, everyone else headed to the strip club, while Rhys and I went to his room at the Luxurian Suites Hotel to hang out alone together. We sat next to each other on the bed in our rumpled suits, our ties loosened, resting against the bed's headboard as we drank beer. I wondered how many more nights we could spend like that after he got married. An impending sense of loss crept up on me in the silence between us.

Rhys interrupted my thoughts. "Luci, am I making a mistake?" He always called me that, which had led to countless people mistaking me for his girlfriend. The only person who that had bothered was Olivia. Well, her and most of our ex-girlfriends.

"Yeah, if you keep drinking, Olivia will lose her shit when you're hungover tomorrow," I answered.

"I meant do you think I'm making a mistake by marrying her?"

He shouldn't have dated her to begin with, but I couldn't bring myself to tell him that. I needed to choose my words carefully, but being drunk made that difficult. I took a long sip to delay answering. "It's a little late in the game to be questioning that now."

"Yeah, you're right. If she didn't kill me for standing her up, her mom definitely would."

"I certainly wouldn't want to get on Sharron's bad side."

Rhys tilted his head back against the bed and looked at the ceiling with a heavy sigh. "I wonder how many miserable Christmases I'll have to spend with her asshole parents before they convince Olivia that she's too good for me?"

"If you ask me, it's the other way around. You're awesome and funny, not to mention way smarter than her."

"Don't forget sexy as fuck," he reminded me with a cheeky grin.

My gaze drifted over Rhys's stretched-out legs crossed at the ankles, over his lithe body, then up to his ridiculously handsome face. While his chiseled cheekbones and strong jaw were attractive, his gray-blue eyes were his most striking feature. It was probably weird that

I was a straight guy who thought my best friend had the most beautiful eyes I had ever seen, but it was an objective fact. His sandy-blond hair always had a mussed look, making you want to run your fingers through it. That was probably a weird urge, too. Shit, I was drunker than I thought.

Something stirred inside me as I continued studying Rhys. I blamed the alcohol, but that didn't stop me from agreeing, "And hot as hell."

He grinned at my comment. "Damn right I am." He killed the last of his drink, then leaned over to grab another one off the nightstand.

"Slow down, or else you won't be able to walk in a straight line down the aisle at your rehearsal," I warned. "At this rate, you'll still be hungover on your actual wedding day."

He ignored me as he flipped the cap off the bottle. "Maybe I don't want to go through with it."

I tried not to get my hopes up that he was getting cold feet. "You don't have to get shitfaced to call off the wedding. If you want to walk away from this, you know I've got your back."

He twisted the glass bottle in his hands. "Don't get me wrong. She's hot, but she's not..."

I had never heard him question his relationship with Olivia before. It took an effort to not get excited that he may back out of the wedding before it was too late. "She's not what?"

"She's not you, Luci."

It took a moment for his comment to process through

my sluggish mind, but I decided it was too weird. I confiscated his beer bottle. "You're talking crazy, so I'm cutting you off."

Rhys laughed and grabbed his drink back from me, sloshing some on the sheets. "I meant she doesn't get me like you do. I can tell you anything, and you won't judge me for it. Olivia judges me about *everything*."

"In fairness, she judges everyone about everything." I made another attempt to steal away his drink but failed. "It's not just you."

His grin slid into a sad smile that pained my drunk heart. "It's not fair."

"What's not?"

"I wouldn't have to marry Olivia if you were a girl."

"Seriously, give me your beer." I held out my hand to take it from him. "You've officially had *way* too much to drink."

He refused to comply. "I'm being serious. I would have married you years ago if you had been a girl. When you think about it, we're perfect for each other. We tell each other everything, and we have the same sense of humor. Plus, I'm man enough to admit that you're good-looking and I'm happiest when I'm with you."

"That's just your cold feet talking."

Rhys pinned me under his intense gaze. "You don't agree?"

The longer he looked at me, the more flustered I became. I was sober enough to realize our conversation was heading in a dangerous direction, but too drunk to get things back on track. The truth was too embarrassing to admit out loud. I nervously adjusted my glasses. "It's hard to claim we're perfect for each other when you're forgetting that whole 'we can't fuck each other because we're straight' part."

He crooked his finger and used it to lift my chin up, forcing our gazes to meet. "It's not like we haven't kissed."

I was in a free fall as Rhys stared at me with his hypnotizing eyes. We never talked about the fact that we were each other's first kiss and not Tara Robinson like everyone thought. Our attempts at practicing kissing to prepare for being with girls was something I had locked away deep inside my soul. It was far too dangerous to remember, because I had enjoyed it more than I should have. It had confused me for years why making out with girls had never made me feel the same sparks that kissing Rhys had. I had written it off as romanticizing the magic of my first kiss, because that's all it could ever be.

My heart pounded as I desperately tried to stay out of trouble. "It was one time."

Rhys's voice dropped lower, sending a shiver through me. "No, it wasn't. We've pleasured each other before, too."

The memory of us experimenting with jerking each other off one summer night was another thing I had repressed to preserve our friendship. It was the first time in years I had thought about it. Remembering it even now still made me hot and bothered. "Once, and my sister interrupted us before we finished. It doesn't count."

Rhys ran his thumb against my lower lip. "I was

leaning in to kiss you when she interrupted us, remember?"

Oh, I remembered. I remembered I wanted it so much that it had terrified me then, and that fear never went away. Especially since that same stupid part of my heart I had spent years ignoring yearned for Rhys to make a move on me. I couldn't force myself to move away like I should. I could only whisper, "You're getting married."

"Olivia cut me off six months ago so that our honeymoon would be 'special' for her." His tongue darted out to lick his lips, drawing my attention to them. "That's why I'm alone in this room and not with her in the honeymoon suite. Shit, I'm so fucking horny. It's not cheating if it's with a guy, right?"

"Yes, it is," I argued, even as my blood rushed south at the unforgivable idea. "You're better than that. We both are."

"Come on, we're two grown men. It'd just be a mutual hand job, not sex."

My dick perked up at the offer, but I shut it down. "I'm not risking Olivia banning me from ever seeing you again when she finds out."

"She'll never find out," Rhys promised, weaving a dangerous entrapment spell on me. "It'll be our little secret. After all, what happens in Vegas, stays in Vegas, right?"

"We're not having this conversation." It was too much of a threat to our relationship. The only way to maintain the status quo in our friendship was to get drunk enough that I wouldn't remember anything in the morning.

The sultry fire in Rhys's expressive eyes was seductive as he trailed his fingers down my neck. I trembled with confused desire when he asked, "Haven't you ever wondered what it would be like if we hooked up?"

I couldn't admit that I had imagined it in the past—had even gotten off on the fantasy—before I banished the memories when I was a teenager. He was my best friend, so I refused to imagine him like that. No, I only liked women—despite how long it had been since I had slept with one. That had to be the reason he was swaying me in my inebriated stupor. It couldn't be because my dumbass heart had secretly been longing for him since we were teenagers.

"Why did we never try again?"

"Because it was a mistake," I insisted, attempting to convince him as much as myself.

"Was it?"

Rhys leaned closer, making me tense. Instead of kissing me, he rested his head on my shoulder, draping himself over my chest, careful not to spill his drink. My free hand embraced him, devastating me with how right it felt. His hardness pressed against my thigh, causing my cock to stiffen in response. It made me want things I could never have.

"If it's so wrong, why does being with you always feel so right?" Rhys wondered, echoing my own traitorous thoughts. "Why do I want tonight to last forever with you so that tomorrow never comes?"

They were questions I didn't have an answer to, despite feeling the same way.

"Am I the only one who feels like this?"

Without having to look into his bewitching storm-colored eyes, it was easier to admit, "No."

"Luci."

Rhys moaned my name like a physical caress, arousing me more than it should have. I bit my lip to hold in the noise that wanted to escape, fully erect in an instant. "We can't do this. Stop for both of our sakes, before we do something you'll regret."

"Why would I regret it?"

Our conversation was too fucking weird to be okay. I reminded him, "You love Olivia, remember?"

"But I love you more."

Although he didn't mean it romantically, his words hit me hard. The fluttering of his long eyelashes and lips ghosting against my neck made me quiver with a misguided desire. It confused my heart. I sounded unbearably sad when I countered, "It's not the same thing." No, he would never love me like that. I wasn't supposed to want that, either. So why did it hurt?

"We lose all plausible deniability of 'no homo' when we're both this turned on." He laughed, but I couldn't do the same.

"It's the beer's fault," I argued, refusing to acknowledge that my hard-on had more to do with Rhys than the alcohol. "It means nothing."

He sat back up and downed the rest of his bottle. "I guess we should keep drinking until we get whiskey dick so I don't give Olivia another reason to complain I'm ruining 'her' wedding."

I finished my drink. "You can't get whiskey dick from drinking beer."

Rhys grabbed two more bottles from the nightstand, cracking them both open before giving me one. "Fine, drunk dick."

It didn't escape my notice that his gaze dropped to the noticeable tent in my pants, causing my cheeks to burn as I did the same to him. What the hell were we doing?

Rather than commenting on it, he held his bottle out to toast. "Does my best man have anything to say on behalf of his groom?"

I got hung up on Rhys saying he was my groom. It made it sound like I was the one marrying him. I raised my drink up, wracking my brain to come up with something appropriate. "I wish you a lifetime of wedded bliss."

"Cheers!" Rhys clinked his beer against mine. After we both took a sip, he started to laugh. "I need to marry someone else for your wish to come true, though."

"It's not too late. I mean, it's Vegas. There are twenty-four-hour Elvis wedding chapels everywhere," I joked. "All you need is someone willing."

"God, can you imagine the look of Olivia's face if I did that?" Rhys asked, cackling with laughter. "It would almost be worth it."

I laughed along with him. "I guess it depends on who you're stuck with after eloping."

"Yeah, that would go over *real* well." He snorted, before mimicking a conversation with his fiancée. "Sorry, babe, but they let me walk down the aisle to an Elvis impersonator singing, 'Just a hunk, a hunk of burning love,' instead of that stupid wedding march song. You can see why I had to marry them, right?"

I chuckled. "That would be hilarious, but I doubt she'd see the humor in it."

"Hey, I could set her up with the Elvis impersonator afterward so she doesn't kill me for ditching her at the altar last-minute."

"She's more interested in having a wedding than being married, so it might work."

"You're not wrong," he agreed with a wry grin. "Plus, she loves shiny stuff, and most of the Elvis impersonators are pretty blinged out, so it'd be a match made in heaven. I'd be doing us both a huge favor. You know, I think I'm onto something here."

"I'm about two beers away from this being a great idea," I retorted, guzzling most of mine in a single swig.

Rhys chugged the rest of his beer, before grabbing another from the dwindling supply on the nightstand. "Oh, it's on!"

My competitive streak trounced the last shred of common sense I had left that night. "Challenge accepted."

That proved to be a huge mistake.

Chapter 2

Rhys Huntington

I regretted waking up in the morning. The pounding in my skull felt like someone had borrowed my brain for their timpani drums practice, keeping time with every beat of my heart. My mouth was dryer than the Sahara Desert and tasted like death. I had sandpaper in my throat when I swallowed. When I opened my eyes, the rays of light streamed through the windows and stabbed my retinas like it was a personal attack.

With a whimper, I closed my eyes to surround myself in darkness once more. It caused me to burrow closer to the warm body I had curled up against, resting my head on their shoulder. The arm holding me protectively was the only good thing about existing right now. Everything else hurt like hell. I wished I could sleep off the worst hangover I had had since college. *Why did I drink so much last night?*

My first sign that all was not as it should be was when the person I was using as a pillow groaned—a deep and masculine rumbling. In my drunken stupor, I had assumed I was sleeping with Olivia. However, as my hand glided up a very naked and flat chest, I realized I was mistaken.

"Luci?" I croaked.

His hand resting on my hip twitched as he rasped, "Yeah?"

"God, I feel like shit." I sagged against him. I should have moved away, but I wasn't even sure if I was capable of it at the moment.

"That makes two of us."

The sound of his gravelly morning voice went straight to my dick. I didn't have the wherewithal to control that part of me when an army of assholes with knives on their boots tap-danced in my brain. It got worse when Luci's fingers absentmindedly caressed me, arousing me and drawing attention to the fact that I was naked—that we were *both* naked. Everything hurt too much to think about why.

"Fuck, the rehearsal," he reminded me.

I knew I wasn't late for it, because Olivia would have been pounding on the door and reaming me a new asshole if I was. With monumental effort, I brought my left hand up to rub my eye, grimacing when I felt an unfamiliar sensation of metal against my skin. *What the hell?*

It was weird enough to get me to open my eyes again, squinting as the sun assaulted me for my stupidity. I furrowed my eyebrows in confusion when I saw I had on my wedding ring, a black tungsten band with a rose-gold groove in the center. When the hell had I put it on—and more importantly, *why?*

An image flashed through my mind of Luci sliding the wedding band onto my finger, which sent a jolt of adrenaline through me. It gave me the burst of energy I needed, but it was like moving through quicksand as I struggled to sit up. The wave of nausea that crashed into me made me press the heel of my palms against my eyes until it passed. I waited until I was certain I wouldn't throw up before I lowered my hands.

I got flustered by the sight of the sheets dipping low on Luci's hips, his dark hair falling in front of his handsome face. It was a rare treat for me to see him without his glasses on, but it *really* wasn't the right time to appreciate that my best friend was attractive.

When he rubbed his eyes, my stomach lurched at the sight of Olivia's wedding ring of two alternating rows of round and baguette diamonds on his ring finger. He had always hated how feminine his long, slim fingers were, and being nearly the same size as Olivia's annoyed him almost as much as she resented it. I secretly thought his hands were beautifully elegant like a pianist's, but the presence of my fiancée's ring set off my rising panic. "What's the last thing you remember?"

His bleary gaze focused on me with an effort. "Wait, why are you naked?"

"Why are *you* naked?" Another surge of foreboding flooded through me as a memory of Luci's hands running down my bare spine to cup my ass flickered in my mind. "Lucien, what the fuck did we do last night?" I had progressed to freaking out, because I only used his full name when I was scared or serious.

Eyebrows drawing together in thought, he answered in a questioning tone, "We were celebrating your marriage?"

I was unprepared for being blindsided by remembering kissing Luci at the altar. To stop everything from spinning out, I pressed my palm my forehead to steady myself. "Please tell me we didn't do what I think we did."

His blue eyes were full of confusion as he looked at my wedding band, then lifted his hand to see he was wearing Olivia's. He squinted at it before fumbling for his glasses on the nightstand. After a long look, his voice trembled when he said, "I don't think I can."

"This can't be happening." I tried not to hyperventilate as scenes from our drunken night replayed in broken fragments. Us laughing as we filled out paperwork at the chapel, exchanging our rings, our passionate kiss in the presence of the Elvis impersonator minister. Then, us making out in the limo on the ride back to the hotel, popping a bottle of champagne, our clothes coming off as we fooled around until we lost our nerve and passed out from being too drunk. "Holy shit, Olivia is going to kill us both. God, we're so fucked."

"No, because if we only had a ceremony in a chapel, we're not *legally* married," Luci pointed out. "To make it official, we would have needed—"

"A marriage license."

We stared at each other in horror. Everything moved in slow motion as I remembered standing in the marriage license office, complaining that there shouldn't be a line that late at night on a Thursday. Desperate for some kind of evidence to the contrary, I scrambled for my phone to check for any clues.

The world went sideways when I saw an email from the Clark County Clerk's Office confirming our online marriage license pre-application submission. A receipt from the Grand Chapel of Graceland was next. I had irrefutable proof that we had purchased the VIP wedding package, including the ceremony, rental tuxedos, flowers, photographs, and round-trip transportation to the Marriage License Bureau, then back to our hotel. No matter how many times I read that we could pick up the souvenir copy of our marriage certificate and photographs later, it didn't make sense. How could my best friend now legally be my husband?

Dropping my phone, I doubled over with my head in my hands. "Fuck, I'm going to be sick."

I officially had the hangover from hell.

Chapter 3

Luci

It had to be a joke, right? We couldn't really be *that* stupid, could we?

Unfortunately, between wearing Olivia's wedding ring and my hangover, I had ample evidence to the contrary. Shit, I was *way* too hungover to deal with any level of crisis. Even though I wanted to pull the covers over my head and pretend none of this was happening, I sat up to deal with our massive fuckup. My vision swam, the room spinning a little from my residual buzz.

Once it passed, I picked up Rhys's phone to see what had caused him to react that way. It took some effort to make my eyes focus on the words, but nothing could have prepared me for seeing a visual confirmation about our accidental nuptials. My disbelief was at war with the fear bubbling up inside of me.

I protested, "This is just a bill for the ceremony. It's not legally binding if—"

Without looking at me, Rhys miserably said, "The next email is our marriage license pre-application confirmation from the County Clerk's Office."

That tore the last shred of hope from me. "Shit."

We fell silent as we realized the enormity of our situation. I closed my eyes, trying to remember the previous night. We had been joking about Rhys getting married in one of those quickie marriage chapels, laughing as we drank and looked online at the craziest ones in Vegas. It had seemed like a hilarious idea at the time when he suggested we go check it out in person.

The walk over sobered us up as Rhys confessed that he was only marrying Olivia because it was what he felt like he should do after being with her for so long. It intensified my selfish hope he would call off the wedding, that maybe I wouldn't lose him to her. Thus, when he announced to the chapel receptionist that we were there to get married, I had played along out of curiosity.

Left alone to fill out our paperwork, I had asked him how far he was planning on taking the joke. I never expected to hear him say, "If I'm spending the rest of my life with only one person, I want it to be you, Luci. Marry me."

The word "no" hadn't even crossed my mind.

After filling out applications, they drove us to the Marriage License Bureau. Just like we had talked about at the hotel, Rhys sauntered down the aisle to an Elvis impersonator singing "Burning Love." It had seemed like a funny joke, but the magnitude of the moment had hit me as we exchanged rings. Our first kiss as husbands awoke something within me that had been slumbering since that night when we were awkward teenagers experimenting with each other.

After that, it was like a dam had burst inside us both.

We made out in the limo, making up for all the years we hadn't kissed. I recalled celebrating with champagne in our room, giving us the boldness to strip each other in between nervous laughs, but we ended up losing our nerve in the face of being drunk off our asses. There was a conflicting sense of relief and disappointment that we hadn't been intimate with each other. That's when the reality hit me all over again that *holy shit, we're legally husbands*.

"What the fuck am I supposed to do?" Rhys demanded, a note of hysteria in his voice. "Can't we get this annulled or something?"

The question hurt, even though it shouldn't have. "Probably, but I don't know how long that takes."

"If we got the marriage license in under an hour, how hard can it be to undo it? We can just say we were drunk."

"Except we were pretty much sober by that point," I pointed out. "We didn't get wasted until we came back to the hotel afterward." I sure as hell was never drinking champagne again.

He waved away the concern. "The court won't know that." He picked up his phone and started researching our options, but it didn't take long before the color drained from his face. "Fuck, fuck, fuck!"

"What?"

"It can take up to three weeks for them to grant an annulment," Rhys answered, looking up at me with a frightened expression. "The 'we were a little drunk and made a mistake' defense isn't a solid legal ground for one."

"That can't be right."

"This site says you have to present witnesses to show you didn't have a clue about what you were doing. Plus, a chapel can't let you get married if you're too drunk to consent. What are we going to do, Lucien? Tell me what we have to do!"

I knew things were bad when he called me by my full name. He had a tendency to panic, so I was used to staying calm for the both of us. "Look, we'll figure something out."

"By tomorrow?" His voice cracked in his fear. "Did you not hear the part where I said an annulment takes up to *three weeks* to process?"

"If it's up to three weeks, it could also take less time than that," I pointed out, trying to find a way to alleviate his anxiety.

"Even one week is still too long," he argued.

He was right, but his words made me realize something that would only make the problem worse. "Oh, fucking hell."

"What?"

I gestured between us as I explained, "Regardless of how we feel about it, in the eyes of the law, we're legally married. That means if you go through with the wedding and marry Olivia tomorrow, you'd void your marriage with her since you're really married to me. You'd also be committing bigamy, which is illegal, and they can arrest you for it."

Rhys threw himself facedown with a frustrated noise. "What do I tell Olivia? Her family? *My* family? *Your* family? God, how did I fuck this up so much? Shit, shit, shit!"

"This isn't all on you." I paused midair when I reached out to comfort him like I normally would. Under the circumstances, it didn't seem wise. *Neither was marrying him*, my brain oh-so-helpfully reminded me far too late.

"Yeah, but it was *my* idea." He groaned into the sheets.

"That I agreed to."

He faced me once again. "Why did you?"

Before I could answer, Rhys's phone rang. We both swore when Olivia's name popped up on the display.

"Fuck, what do I do?" His eyes begged me to help him. "Tell me what to do!"

"Answer it. If you don't, she'll come in here. We have enough problems right now without that."

Rhys grumbled, before he accepted the call on speakerphone with a gruff, "Hey, babe."

"Wow, you're actually awake?" Olivia asked in sarcastic amazement. Her tone set me on edge. "I'm impressed. I assumed I would have to drag you out of bed for breakfast."

"No, I'm up," Rhys told her, "but I still need to get ready."

"Well, hurry it the fuck up, because breakfast is at eight thirty," Olivia ordered, causing me to cringe. I hated how she always bossed him around like that. "You better not embarrass me, Leopold." I also couldn't stand the fact that she called Rhys by his legal name which he hated. It was beyond me why he tolerated that.

We shared a guilty look. "I'm hopping in the shower now. I'll see you downstairs."

"Fine," Olivia replied in a clipped tone, abruptly hanging up.

Even after being together for over three years and one day away from being his wife, Olivia never ended a call with "I love you." It bothered me now more than ever.

He tossed his phone aside in disgust before hiding his face again with a sob. "I can't do this!"

"I'll go with you."

He sarcastically shot back, "Yeah, because that will go over *really* well when you show up wearing Olivia's wedding ring."

"I can take it off." When I attempted to, I discovered that I couldn't remove it. I sat up to try again, but no matter how hard I pulled or twisted it, the ring wouldn't go over my knuckle. "Shit, it's stuck."

"Of course it is."

"No, I'm serious," I told him, the strain clear in my voice as I continued struggling to force off the band. I was close to Olivia's ring size, but apparently not close enough. It refused to budge. I didn't have the luxury of time to be amused by the fact that for the first time in my life, I wished my fingers were slimmer. "Damn, how did you even get this thing on me?"

"Here, let me try."

I held my hand out to him, having déjà vu from when he had slid the ring on my finger last night. That faded fast when he yanked on it. I gritted my teeth against the pain, but after a fierce tug, I swore, "Ow, shit! That really hurts."

"Sorry," Rhys reflexively apologized, not letting go yet.

"It's okay."

He brushed his thumb against the back of my knuckles, sending a shiver through me. The corner of his mouth turned up into a slight smirk. "I guess it's a good thing it suits you, because that thing's not coming off."

"It's kind of flashy for my tastes," I joked, relieved that Rhys's panic had subsided.

He chuckled at my comment. "What are you talking about? You picked it out, remember?"

Rhys hadn't had the first clue what kind of jewelry to buy, so I had helped him pick out rings for him and Olivia. The diamond band with the two rows of alternating round and baguette stones had caught my eye. It was by far the shiniest ring in the store, which I had assumed Olivia would appreciate. When Rhys had made me try it on in the store, I never in a million years expected I'd be wearing it someday for real.

My lips quirked into a grin. "I guess we shouldn't have made fun of the jeweler for initially assuming we were the ones getting married, huh?"

"Looks like Cathy got the last laugh," Rhys replied.

"Well, on the bright side, at least I had the good sense to elope with you. I'd be on the bridge if I had married Ambrose."

While Ambrose was a close friend of ours and one of Rhys's groomsmen, he was an unrepentant womanizer. His charming Irish accent and handsome face had broken countless hearts. "See? It could always be worse."

"I'm not sure this is the right occasion for optimism," he said, but a smile tugged at his lips.

"Are you going to be okay?"

Rhys didn't answer me as he continued studying my hand. He toyed with the ring but made no further attempts at removing it. When he looked up at me, there was a storm of worries in his eyes. "As long as we're okay."

"We're still good," I promised. "Whatever you need to do, you know I'm there for you."

"Thank god." He sighed in relief. "I don't know what I would have done if I had fucked up my engagement and our friendship in the same night."

"No matter what, you're always my best friend."

Rhys added in bemusement, "And your husband. How weird is that?"

"Super weird, but we should get ready before Olivia comes barging in on us naked in bed together. That would be *way* harder to explain."

He grimaced. "For what it's worth, I'm sorry that I drug you into this mess."

I'm not, I realized with a start. It was a thought I was too overwhelmed to comprehend. Instead of reflecting on it, I tried to cheer up Rhys. "I'm sure we'll look back on this someday and laugh."

"Provided Olivia doesn't murder us at breakfast first." He started to move toward the edge of the bed but paused.

When he glanced back at me with a consternated expression, I realized his dilemma. "You're embarrassed about me seeing you naked, aren't you?" I laughed. "Why? This isn't the first time I've seen you like this."

"It's different now," Rhys protested.

"Yeah, now it's legally sanctioned." That fact equally amused and bewildered me.

"For now." His words once again cut me deep without meaning to. He was unsteady on his feet as he stood up, but he staggered to the bathroom with a pained groan.

I was a horrible person for checking out him out, and I got my comeuppance for the mistake when he smirked over his shoulder. My cheeks were flame red as he joked, "I can't say I'm surprised. You've always been an ass man."

"Sorry," I mumbled, feeling like an asshole for appreciating the view. In my defense, an ass was an ass, regardless if it was a man or a woman. And Rhys certainly had a nice one.

"I'll take the compliment." He disappeared into the bathroom.

I took off my glasses and flopped onto my back. With a heavy sigh, I slung my arm over my eyes to block out the light that was still much too bright for a hangover. How had everything become such a mess?

As tempting as it was to lie there and try to figure out what we could do about this crazy problem, I had to get dressed. Sorting out my feelings for Rhys would have to wait until later.

Chapter 4

Rhys

TRUE TO HIS WORD, Luci stayed with me so we could address Olivia together. As we rode the elevator down to breakfast, I checked my reflection in the mirrored walls. Despite feeling like shit, I looked halfway decent in my jeans and black sweater. I chose a dark color in case Olivia threw her Bloody Mary at me in a fit of rage over my announcement.

I glanced over at Luci, amazed at how refreshed he appeared considering he was as hungover as me. His button-down maroon shirt with light acid-washed jeans flattered his athletic build. His muscles had always seemed at odds with his nerdy square glasses and gentle spirit. He didn't appear like someone who had spent the night drunk off his ass making bad decisions. With his thumbs tucked into his front pockets, Olivia's wedding band sent cascades of sparkles against the walls.

The plummeting of my stomach had little to do with how fast the elevator was descending. How had we ended up married for real? Plenty of people had teased us about being an old married couple, and we were in some respects. However, it was one thing to joke about it; it was another thing for it to be true—especially right before my *actual* wedding with my fiancée.

No matter how much I wished I could blame the alcohol, I couldn't. Sure, Olivia had a banging hot body, but she was pretentious, haughty, and superficial to an obnoxious degree. We may have claimed to love each other, but she only loved that I was rich enough to give her the luxurious lifestyle she expected. The prospect of living in a loveless marriage like my parents suffocated me.

I should have broken up with her years ago. However, I had been so tired of the endless parade of sycophantic beauties only interested in my family. It had been easier to stay with her than find a new girlfriend. They all ended up being the same anyway, so what difference did it make?

It helped that my folks liked her, although I suspected my asshole father's interest in her was far from pure, given his history of chasing after younger women. The same wasn't true in reverse, because Olivia's parents couldn't stand me.

She had been engaged to some hotshot financial bro in Massachusetts before we dated. Her parents never let me forget that I could never compare to Chaz, even if I cared to try. He had cheated on Olivia with her close friend and gotten her knocked up, so it shouldn't have been a competition. Yet somehow, he came out on top with her folks. After ruining Olivia's big day, I'd definitely be the bad guy. I suppose it should bother me, but I was out of fucks to give.

After dating over three years, marriage had been the next logical step. As the wedding planning started, I kept expecting our relationship to fall apart since we weren't in love. It wasn't until my bachelor party that I fully understood I was on the verge of being trapped in a life I never wanted.

When I was sitting in my room with Luci afterward, it occurred to me I had never had a girlfriend who I loved more than him. The alcohol made me bold, and my fear of losing him to Olivia made me stupid. I vividly remembered telling him he was the only person I wanted to spend the rest of my life with—and I still meant it. I'd rather wed my platonic soul mate instead of her.

Except things hadn't been very platonic after our impromptu ceremony. Our kisses had been more passionate than any I had ever shared with a girlfriend before. I hadn't imagined that we both had been hard and wanting. I wondered if Luci had experienced the same all-consuming desire to be together. Maybe I was the only weird one.

One thing I knew for sure was that I shouldn't have jerked off this morning because I was so turned on by him enjoying checking out my ass. Even now, my cock responded to the memories. I shifted on my feet as I tried to put such thoughts out of my mind. The last thing I needed was another confusing erection inspired by Luci.

While I dreaded Olivia going off on me for doing this to her the day before our wedding, I was more afraid Luci wouldn't forgive me. He was too nice to tell me no, and I had used that to my advantage like a total asshole. Although he had been understanding so far, he had every right to be angry with me for betraying our friendship. If he decided he never wanted to see me again, I'd deserve it for persuading him to marry me against his better judgment.

I would be fine after my fight with Olivia, but my heart clenched at the thought of Luci hating me. Out of everything, he was the sole thing I couldn't bear to lose. It would be like losing the other half of myself, the very thought of it making it hard to breathe in the small space of the elevator.

The doors pinged open. I blindly followed him out, a family of four getting on after us. Instead of exiting at the restaurants, we were on a random hotel room floor. I looked up at him in confusion.

He held my shoulders, gazing down at me with so much concern, that in my unbalanced state, it brought tears to my eyes. How could he look at me like that after what I had forced him to do?

Luci's voice was warm and gentle as he assured me, "It's okay, Rhys. Just breathe."

I was hyperventilating again, on the brink of a panic attack—not because I'd married Luci, but because my stupidity costing me our friendship terrified me. I stared up at him with all my fear and confusion, needing him to understand so he could make it better. He always knew the right thing to say or do in every situation.

When he gathered me into a hug, I threw my arms

around him and clung to him. "I'm so sorry, Luci. Please don't hate me!"

"I'm not mad at you, Rhys. I couldn't hate you if I tried." Luci's words soothed me almost as much as being in his embrace did. It was the only place in the world I was safe and loved. How had I never noticed that before? "You don't have to be sorry. We're in this together, remember?"

The fact that I'd rather stay in Luci's arms than see my fiancée told me everything I needed to know in that moment. There would be no begging for Olivia's forgiveness, no pleading for another chance, no promises that I would annul my marriage if only she'd have me. I may have eloped with my best friend on a whim, but it was shaping up to be my smartest relationship decision ever.

I stepped back and took a shuddering breath, running my fingers through my hair as I steadied myself. Luci was the most understanding person in the world. There wasn't a problem we couldn't move past. He might be mad at me for a little while once the dust settled, but he would forgive me. This would be okay. We would be okay.

"Hey, you're still wearing your wedding ring," he pointed out. "I thought you were leaving it in the room?"

That had been my original intention, because it minimized the chances of a confrontation over breakfast. However, I knew on a subconscious level why I'd left it on to confront Olivia. With a shrug, I walked over to the elevators and pressed the down button. "I changed my mind."

"We don't have to do this now," he offered. "If you prefer to wait until you talk to her alone in private, or—"

I stopped him. "I'll play it by ear. Whatever happens, happens."

There were no more words as we went to face off against my fiancée.

OLIVIA WAS WAITING OUTSIDE of the restaurant, tapping her stiletto heel on the floor. Her pink dress was so short that it amazed me she would wear it in front of her family at breakfast. Her breasts almost spilled out of the top of it, which was earning her quite a few looks as other people walked by her. Her bun was so tight my headache got worse from looking at it. She was artificially beautiful, but there wasn't an ounce of kindness in her piqued expression.

After she had declared no sex until our honeymoon, seeing her in that outfit should have filled me with an urge to fuck her where she stood. Instead, I was devoid of any desire for her. Somehow, waking up naked next to Luci that morning had turned me on more. Not to mention that I masturbated in the shower thinking about him and not her. Those were dangerous thoughts, so I pushed it aside to handle later.

When I saw how pissed off Olivia looked, I glanced at my watch. We were five minutes early for breakfast. Before we approached her, I shoved my hands in my pockets to hide my ring, noticing Luci had done the same.

"Where the fuck have you been, Leopold?" she hissed once we were close enough to hear her.

I hated that she only called me by my first name. It emphasized how she only cared about my family legacy, rather than about me. I had tried to make her stop in the beginning, but at some point, I had given up the fight. I was such an idiot for wasting so much time with her. Why didn't I realize that until it was almost too late?

Frowning at the greeting, I asked, "What the hell is your problem? Chill, we're not late."

"Don't tell me to chill!" Olivia snapped. "And why is *he* here?"

The disgust in her tone as she pointed at Luci with a hateful glare made my blood boil with rage. I could deal with any insults aimed at me, but I refused to tolerate her treating him like shit. "*He* is here because he's my best man."

"So?"

"Your maid of honor is here, so it's only fair."

"That's because Katie's my sister! This breakfast is family only. Lucien, leave."

I appreciated that he didn't obey her. With a nonplussed shrug, I said, "If you won't let him join us, I'll order room service with him instead. Have fun with your folks."

When I turned away, she grabbed my upper arm, her acrylic nails digging into my bicep. "You're such a pain in the ass, you know that?"

"How could I forget when you remind me every

chance you get?" I asked, shaking her off me. "What's your problem?"

She crossed her arms over her chest and lifted her breasts higher. Her brown eyes were full of accusations. "Ambrose and Katie broke up yesterday."

"So? That's the third time this month. They'll be back together before the rehearsal dinner tonight."

"He cheated on her with a stripper," Olivia spat, glaring at Luci as if he had something to do with it. "They're done for good this time."

"Hey, we weren't there. Ambrose went to a strip club without us, so it's not our fault." The irony that I would have gotten in less trouble there than drinking alone with Luci would have been funny under any other circumstance. "Try being thankful that there'll be less drama now."

"I'm sick of this bullshit! Ambrose is out of my wedding!"

I started to argue she couldn't kick out one of my groomsmen, but it didn't matter when there wouldn't be a wedding. "Okay."

The stunned expression on Olivia's face was comical as she sputtered, "O-okay? What do you mean '*okay*'?"

"As in, okay, Ambrose doesn't have to be in the wedding anymore," I patronizingly clarified. "That's what you want, isn't it?"

"You won't fight me on it?"

I didn't blame her for looking suspicious. "Do you want me to?"

"Of course not!"

"What's your issue, then?"

Olivia frowned at me as she accused me, "You don't care at all, do you?"

"As you've repeatedly told me, this is *your* wedding. In your own words, I'm just supposed to shut up and show up, right?" Ha, fat chance of that happening now. "Is there anything else? Because we're all late now thanks to you."

"God, I fucking hate you sometimes," she muttered under her breath.

"Only sometimes? Huh, it must be true what they say about absence making the heart grow fonder." That wasn't the case for me, since having distance from her showed me why I should stay away permanently.

With a final glare, she turned on her heel and stormed inside.

I grinned as I bumped Luci with my shoulder. "See? It's going great."

"Why didn't you fight her about Ambrose?" His eyebrows creased in confusion. "If he's out, you know August will bail, too."

Luci was right. He always was. Much like our relationship, Ambrose and August were an inseparable duo. He had long suspected there was more to their friendship, but I found it hard to believe given Ambrose's love of the ladies. The man was aggressively heterosexual. Besides, August had almost as many women in his bed. Then again, weirder things had happened, as our recent marriage proved.

Rather than commenting on that, I pointed out, "She can't kick him out if there's no wedding."

"No wedding?" he repeated in shock. "But I thought—"

I interrupted him by clasping his shoulder with a squeeze. "Don't worry about it. Let's go before she decides her stilettos need to become acquainted with my balls."

He remained unconvinced, but he followed me over to where my folks, Olivia's parents, and her sister waited. She dropped into the chair with a huff and dour scowl.

There were two free seats next to my parents, so I sat next to my irate fiancée, figuring it would be safest if Luci was between me and my mom. While my old man was a prick to everyone, my mother was nice to him most of the time. She wore a black dress that would have been more appropriate at a funeral. Her dark hair was in a fashionable bob, making her appear younger than she was. Well, that and all the plastic surgery.

Despite it being breakfast, my father was in a full suit and tie. I resembled him in looks, but his features were far more severe. The stress of his job had caused him to go prematurely gray. It always amazed me that my image-conscious mother hadn't forced him dye it to give the illusion of youth. Then again, knowing my dad, he wouldn't give a single fuck if she had asked him to do it.

Besides, my father's silver fox look was working for him, given his many flagrant affairs with younger women. Leo earned enough money that my mom never complained, which I had been bitter about growing up.

Their sham marriage had put me off romance. Only now did I realize how badly it had fucked me up with my interchangeable girlfriends. I had settled for Olivia, because love never played into the equation.

Mom greeted us, but Dad sat in stony silence. It surprised me he was there at all, since I had assumed he'd blow the breakfast off to hit the golf course.

We sat down, careful to keep our left hands out of sight. Luci appeared at ease, which helped steady my own nerves. However, I grew irritated by Olivia glaring at him, looking as if she was attempting to set him on fire with her mind.

I nudged her under the table as I mouthed, "Stop it."

She huffed but remained silent.

It was ridiculous to use one hand with such a massive menu, but our predicament didn't leave me with many options. Luci did it with far more grace than me.

The server came over and took our orders. Once he left, Olivia announced, "I've decided that Ambrose will no longer be in my wedding."

I sighed as she once again claimed that it was "her" wedding. In fact, she had never once referred to it as "our" wedding during our entire engagement. That said it all, really.

Tears welled up in Katie's eyes at the mention of Ambrose's name. I hadn't spent a lot of time around Katie, but it was easy to see that she was the polar opposite of her older sister. She was so heartbroken that I pitied her. Ambrose was good at doing that to people.

"I'm sorry," Katie whispered.

"It's not your fault he's an asshole," Olivia callously declared, earning her a reprimand from her father for her language. Regardless of her being twenty-eight, Jerry kept her on a short leash. "Maybe you'll listen to me and stop wasting your time with him."

"He never should have been involved in the first place," her mother stated, her scornful expression mirroring her oldest daughter's. Wearing a white dress with pearls, Sharron's pinched features gave her a general air of bitchiness. Her plastic surgeon wasn't nearly as skilled as my mom's. "Your taste in friends leaves much to be desired, Leopold."

They made my name sound even more pretentious than it was, which was saying something considering I was Leopold Bertram Huntington, III. In a weird way, I was glad they refused to call me by my nickname, Rhys. It was the name I had chosen for myself, but none of them cared about Rhys. All that mattered was the prestige that came with the Huntington fortune.

When Sharron's gaze drifted over to Luci and back to me again, I was about to go off on her for the implied insult. The only thing stopping me was his touch on my knee. It triggered a jarring memory from last night of his fingers trailing up my naked thigh as he stared down at me with desire darkening his blue eyes. I flushed with heat, which I blamed on the hangover. Without meaning to, I traced over his wedding band, which reminded me of what I needed to do. When he pulled away, I suffered a disconcerting sense of loss.

"He'll make better friends once he comes to the

country club," Olivia promised, giving me a warning look that promised, *or else*.

I could barely contain my disgust. Dad had forced us to hobnob there, hanging out with a bunch of rich, old fucks, whose only interest was bankrolling their millions. It bored me to death growing up, becoming increasingly unbearable the older I got. If Olivia and her family thought they could trot me out like a show pony for their bougie friends to mock, they were in for a real surprise.

My indignation faded when I remembered that none of this would matter after I confessed what we did yesterday. The tightness in my chest loosened at the realization that soon I would be free of Olivia and her uppity family forever. I had become so detached from her bullshit that I never realized how much anxiety she instilled in me until now.

She kicked me with an expectant look.

I managed an unenthusiastic "Uh, yeah. Sure. Sounds great."

Luci covered his mouth to hide his grin at my response.

With him at my side, this whole farce was tolerable. Why had I ever believed this was a life I could endure without wanting to jump off the nearest skyscraper? I owed him a massive apology for forcing him to suffer through over three years of watching me endure this nonsense.

"I'll talk to Francisco about getting Leopold set up at the Nantucket Yacht Club once you get settled out there." Jerry shared his wife's just-smelled-shit expression. His thin comb-over was a sad sight. Her dad was a petty man who tried too hard to make people think he had more money than he did. He was the worst.

It annoyed me whenever they talked about me like I wasn't there, so it took a moment for the latter part of his sentence to register in my brain. "Get settled out there?"

"Yes. When we move out there, Daddy will take care of everything."

I repeated with emphasis, "I'm sorry, *move out there*? As in, move out to Nantucket?"

"Well, it'll really be Martha's Vineyard," she corrected me, "but yeah."

I was sick of being broadsided with shocking revelations today. "Why is this the first I'm hearing about this?"

"You didn't expect me to stay in Sunnyside, did you? You know I hate it there."

"But we live there."

"Yes, and after the wedding, we'll live in Nantucket," she informed me in a clipped tone that implied how stupid she thought I was being.

I raised my voice in my outrage, not caring that we were drawing looks from other people. "My whole life is in Sunnyside! I can't just move."

"Oh, don't be so dramatic, Leopold."

"When were you planning on informing me about all of this?"

She continued. "Don't worry, the Nantucket Realtor has taken care of everything out there with the new house, and the Sunnyside one already has a buyer lined up for your place. All you have to do is sign the papers to finalize the deal."

My head was spinning. "You can't sell *my* place! Your name isn't on the deed."

She waved it away. "You should be glad I'm making this easy for you. I know you hate being bothered with this kind of stuff."

"You're not selling my fucking house! I'm not moving to Nantucket, either!"

"Stop, you're causing a scene," she snarled at me.

"Oh, I haven't even *started* making a scene yet."

Once again, Luci squeezed my thigh to calm me. The heat of my quick-fire rage shifted to burning lust in a second, disorienting me from the suddenness of it—and him being the source. *Again.*

It was only after Luci's touch retreated that my brain started working again. I reminded myself that I wasn't marrying Olivia, and I sure as shit wasn't moving to goddamn *Nantucket* with her. It was beyond outrageous that she believed she could uproot my entire existence without having the decency to at least ask me if I was cool with it. What was even more infuriating was I suspected separating me from Luci was her main motive in moving to the East Coast. It would be a cold day in hell before I let that happen.

"Are you done?" Olivia asked in exasperation.

Servers arriving with our food interrupted the feud. I composed myself as best I could, downing my full glass of water hoping it would help me recover from the worst hangover ever. What difference did it make to get fired up now? It didn't stop me from seething over the disrespect they showed for me and Luci, though.

The smell of everyone's breakfast nauseated me, but it wasn't entirely because of my awful hangover. I was the world's biggest idiot. What was wrong with me that I had seriously intended to marry Olivia? Why had I been so willing to accept such a shitty life? I recalled all the times when Luci tried to persuade me that she was wrong for me—and every girlfriend before that. All he ever wanted was the best for me. No one knew me better than him, so why hadn't I listened to him? I added it to the list of things I should apologize to him for later. Thank god he was too much of a nice guy to give me the "I told you so" speech I more than deserved.

I used the saltshaker, before passing it to Luci. He started to reach out for it with his left hand out of habit.

Olivia's fork clattered on her plate and she screeched, "What the *fuck*?"

"Language!" Jerry bellowed. Everyone in the restaurant was paying attention to us at this point. It was a miracle management hadn't come over yet to request that we knock off the theatrics.

It was the only time I had witnessed Olivia ignore her dad. She stared daggers at me instead. "You better have a damn good explanation for what I just saw."

"Wait, what happened?" Sharron questioned, a sentiment echoed by my mother.

"That's what I want to know." She glared at us suspiciously. "Because it sure looked like Lucien was wearing *my wedding ring*."

For a fraction of a second, the coward in me considered laughing it off as two drunk friends goofing off trying on the weddings bands when it got stuck. Thankfully, the sour feeling in my stomach over her earlier behavior knocked some sense into me. No, even after we annulled our marriage, there was no way in hell I would ever crawl back to her after this.

"That's not your wedding ring," I denied.

"Prove it," she challenged. "Show me."

I nodded in silent permission. It was a serious challenge to stop myself from laughing at his casual manner as he picked up his water, his diamond ring sparkling in the light. He took several long swallows to drain his glass while everyone stared with varying degrees of shock. It impressed me how smooth his performance was. He really did have beautifully slender fingers. I thought about them caressing me all over, sending another flare of confused desire through me.

Olivia screeching brought me back to the present. "What the *actual* fuck, guys? That *is* my wedding ring!"

"No, it's his." I took more pleasure in dropping that bombshell than I should have, but it was satisfying payback for that Nantucket bullshit.

I expected her to scream, to throw something, or to jump across the table and try to yank the ring off Luci. What I hadn't been prepared for was for her to slump against her chair, rolling her eyes while snarling, "I fucking knew it!"

"Knew what?" Jerry demanded, his face turning red in his anger.

Pretending to be me, Olivia mockingly said, "Oh, we're not like that, babe. I promise, we're not *gay*—we're 'just friends.' It's not weird that I call him Luci, so everyone assumes he's my girlfriend. It's harmless!" She snorted at her own words. "You're a lying piece of shit, Leopold."

It wasn't worth the effort to stand up for myself. She would believe whatever she wanted, regardless of what I said. All I gained trying to convince her otherwise was a worse migraine. I settled for shrugging. "It's what's best for everyone."

She stared at Luci in disgust. "You must be really proud of yourself for finally claiming him for your own."

"Unlike you, I love him for more than his bank account," he replied, causing my eyes to widen in surprise. Was that an actual confession, or was he only fucking with her as payback?

"And you wonder why I've hated you since day one?" she questioned with contempt.

"I can assure you the feeling was mutual." Luci's comment once again caught me off guard. He had never been Olivia's biggest fan, but it was news to me he hated her. In the past, he had treated her with an aloof politeness, careful not to antagonize her for my sake. Had that all been an act?

She continued raging against Luci. "I'll *never* forgive you for this!"

"Somehow, I think I'll be able to sleep at night," he dryly retorted, his calmness rankling her. "Speaking of which, we need your key to the honeymoon suite, since you won't be using it."

Every jaw dropped, mine included. The audacity of the demand was *magnificent*. I guess I underestimated how pissed he was at her.

"Oh, get fucked."

"I'm planning on it right after you give us your key." Holy hell, that was fucking *hot*. Did he mean it? It was only with a concentrated effort that I remembered I shouldn't be interested.

She spat with all the hatred in her heart, "I hope you choke on his dick and die."

"Olivia!" Jerry snapped, his rage turning him an interesting shade of purple.

Pointing at Luci, she shouted, "He ruined my wedding, Daddy! He's ruined everything!"

"He didn't ruin anything," I defended him. "You should thank him for saving us divorce attorney fees."

"The honeymoon suite key would be an excellent place to start," he added, gesturing with his fingers that she should give it to him. His actions drew attention to the sparkling diamond ring.

It was probably a bad thing, but I loved this catty side of him. It was fun watching him demolish any trace of composure in my now ex-fiancée.

She was apoplectic. Her mask had fallen, leaving her ugliness on full display. It wasn't a good look on her. "Fine, if you want something—here." She pulled off her engagement ring in revulsion to throw it at me.

I caught it, exposing my wedding band in the process.

"There, now Lucien can have that, too. I don't think my dress will fit him, though."

"Is this true?" Sharron asked, looking scandalized as she clutched her pearls.

"Yeah, she's right. I don't have the fake tits to fill out the dress as well as her," Luci deadpanned.

I could have kissed him for that perfect answer. Instead, I howled with laughter as Sharron got the vapors. The absurdity of the situation caused me to laugh harder. Everyone stared at us like we had lost our minds, but it was the first time in god only knows how long that I finally felt free. It was *amazing*.

I jumped at the sound of my dad slamming his hands on the table. I had almost forgotten he was there, until he yelled, "I refuse to sit here and listen to you fags laughing like this is a joke!"

His words slapped me hard, sobering me up fast as he stormed off. My mom rushed after him without a single glance at me. That hurt more than I would have imagined.

"You both need to go. *Now*," Olivia ordered.

"With pleasure. All we need is your key," Luci told her.

Her only response was to flip him off with both hands.

The joke was on her, because the reservation was under my name and I had access to the room without it. I stood up to address her. "If nothing else, I'm at least grateful that you forced me to realize I prefer to be with someone who loves me for more than being a Huntington. Thanks for that."

I savored the image of her mouth dropping open in disbelief as I interlaced my fingers with Luci's and walked away hand in hand with him. As I left Olivia and her awful family behind me with my head held high, I didn't look back once. There was no need to when Luci was with me.

Chapter 5

Luci

"You know Olivia will kill you for this," I warned, sitting on a living room chair in the honeymoon suite we had commandeered after breakfast.

He grinned at me as he plopped down on the sofa. "Hey, this whole thing was *your* idea. A rather brilliant one, I might add. Besides, I packed her bags and had them transferred to my old room, so I'm not being a total dick. She already has the key to that room. Plus, I could have made her pay for a new hotel room and left her shit in the hallway."

"I doubt that will be much of a consolation once she figures out what you've done. Honestly, I'm amazed she hasn't come up here yet."

"She's probably drowning her sorrows with a Bloody Mary or mimosa." He shrugged. "Either that, or she's stuck downstairs listening to Daddy dearest lecturing her about her 'unladylike' swearing and making a scene. Did you see the look on his face when she told you to choke on my dick? It was priceless!"

"I shouldn't have antagonized her as much as I did," I said with a frown. When Olivia revealed she was selling

Rhys's house to move him to the other side of the country, it brought out the petty, possessive side of me. After three years of her making my best friend miserable, getting payback was gratifying, even if it meant I was an asshole.

Rhys shook his head. "No, you were amazing! It was an epic takedown." His expression turned serious. "I didn't realize you were so mad at her about everything."

"Neither did I." My frustrations with Olivia had been there from the start of their relationship. It wasn't until the fight at breakfast that I understood how much I had repressed in the interest of not causing a rift with Rhys. I had been doing that a lot more than I realized.

He sighed. "I should have listened to you before. You told me from the beginning that being with her was a bad idea."

"You deserve someone who loves you for you and isn't with you because you're a Huntington with money."

"I've only had that with one person before."

I pushed my glasses higher up on the bridge of my nose as I reflected on the ridiculously lengthy list of women Rhys had dated. The only ex-girlfriend I remembered who hadn't cared about him being a Huntington had never claimed to love him, but it was the closest guess I had. "Miranda?"

"Actually, I was referring to you."

When our eyes met, breathing became a challenge. There were no words to defend myself or deny the claim. I stared at him like an idiot instead.

"Unless you were bullshitting downstairs?" Rhys added.

While I appreciated him giving me an out, when I saw his guarded vulnerability, it gave me the courage to admit, "Of course not."

"This is the part where I'm supposed to laugh it off and say, 'Just kidding,' but I don't want to," he confessed, dropping his gaze. "I felt invincible at breakfast, because I knew you were there for me."

"I always have and always will be."

Rhys toyed with the fabric of his jeans. "That's why I got so upset in the elevator."

The connection between the two things puzzled me. "I thought you freaked out over going down for breakfast?"

"No, I was scared I would lose your friendship over my fuckup." He still couldn't bring himself to look at me. "I feared you wouldn't forgive me for tricking you into marrying me so I wouldn't have to be with Olivia anymore."

"There were definitely easier ways to call off the wedding," I joked, trying to cheer him up. "But I meant it when I said I'm not mad at you. I have responsibility for this, too. You couldn't have married me if I had said no."

My words seemed to upset him more. "But that's the problem. You're too nice to tell me no, and I took advantage of that. I'm the worst!"

He was correct; in the history of our friendship, I rarely put my foot down and denied him anything. However, I knew that wasn't what had happened. As he berated himself for what we did, my instinctual need to protect him asserted itself. Since he was hell-bent and determined to blame himself for the marriage, I had to fess up to the truth. "Rhys, I said yes because I wanted to. It had nothing to do with me not wanting to tell you no."

"What do you mean?"

It was humiliating to explain, "If you married me, you couldn't marry Olivia. I consented because I didn't want to lose you. Not to her, not to anyone."

"Oh," Rhys breathed in shock.

We sat in silence, both of us reeling from my confession.

The digital lock beeping in error broke the moment. It sounded a second time, causing Olivia to growl, "What the hell?" She tried a third and fourth time before she rattled the handle. "Let me in!"

"Sounds like someone's still mad," he joked in a hushed overtone.

"I can't imagine why," I sarcastically retorted.

After another failed attempt at entering, she kicked the door with frustration. "I swear to god, if you cocksuckers stole my room, you're dead!"

Rhys's lips curled into a playful smile, before he shouted in ecstasy, "Oh, Luci! Yes!"

It took an effort to smother my laughter over his vindictive streak kicking in such a childish manner. Two could play that game, so I followed his lead. "You like that?"

He wantonly cried out, "So much!"

She pounded on the door, yelling at us. "I'll cut both of your dicks off!"

"Let me hear how much," I taunted Rhys, amused we were pissing off Olivia even more.

I had expected him to make fake sex noises, but in true Rhys fashion, he pushed it to the extreme. Instead of merely making sounds, he put on a show as if she could somehow see it. His back arched up as he moaned as if he was having the best sex of his life. It was so realistic that I was rock hard in an instant. Watching his orgasmic expressions while he writhed made me ache to take over for real—especially once I noticed he also had an erection.

"Fuck, you feel so good!" I growled, resisting the urge to touch myself through my jeans.

Olivia slammed both of her fists against the door. "Stop it, you sick fucks!"

"I'm so close," Rhys whimpered, before he ramped up his moans to a fevered pitch. "Luci, please!"

His erotic performance would haunt me forever. His parted lips triggered memories of kissing them. I longed to cover his mouth with mine and delve deep for another taste of his passion. More than that, I ached to press my body against his as we consummated our marriage.

Unable to stop the game, I commanded in a dark rumble, "Come for me, Rhys!"

His lithe body jerked as he shouted my name. I damn near came from the sight of him calling out to me in his very convincing fake orgasm. The primal part of my brain yearned to pin him down so we could continue. Him looking freshly fucked an in need of ravishing tested my willpower. I didn't dare move, too fearful I would trigger my climax.

The experience forced me to acknowledge I was as hard as a diamond and ready to fuck my best friend. I needed him to moan my name again as I made him come undone, and not just as a game to piss off his ex. I longed to kiss and caress him in a way that was anything but platonic.

That's when I realized, "Uh, I think she left."

Rhys grinned as he ruffled his hair. "Well, that was fun."

"I guess that's one word for it," I muttered, finding it disconcerting we were both still aroused. What did it mean that Rhys had gotten hard while pretending I was fucking him? What did it mean that *I* did? He pulled me from my musing when he started laughing. "What?"

He stretched, forcing me to notice his body. "I can't believe fake fucking you was better than fucking her for real."

"Seriously?" I arched an eyebrow at the claim.

"Let's just say I haven't enjoyed sex that much in a very long time," Rhys replied. "My guess is she went downstairs to the concierge to convince them to let her in here. She'll be back up here to yell at us again when they refuse. Want to get out of here for a while?"

I was ready to agree to anything that meant I wouldn't have to address the realizations he had cursed me with. "Sure."

"I'll use the master bathroom if you want to use that one."

The instant he was out of the room, I bolted for the bathroom. I braced myself against the wall for support, then yanked my pants down to take my hardness in hand. Desperate for relief, I roughly jerked off to the memory of Rhys undulating on the couch. I took it a step further by imagining him masturbating in my fantasy. The knowledge that he was probably doing the same thing right now pushed me to the edge of desire. I whimpered his name as I orgasmed.

Groaning, I banged my head on the wall. How was it possible to feel so good and simultaneously so awful? It was a relief to climax, but I felt dirty for thinking of my best friend to do it. I hadn't done that since I was a teenager. It was the reason I had banished those kinds of thoughts about him to the darkest corner of my heart to ignore forever. But I couldn't unsee what Rhys looked like in the throes of passion or unhear his sounds of pleasure. I didn't know how to live with that knowledge without driving myself insane.

I looked down at my cum-covered hand in disgust. Inside my mind, traitorous whispers reminded me he *was* my husband, so there was nothing wrong with us using the honeymoon suite for its intended purpose. But we were married in name only. Him deciding not to get back together with Olivia didn't mean he would stay with me. He still wanted the annulment. Why did that thought hurt?

Rhys was right about the fact I could never tell him no, but this was the one time I wished I could. There was no way I would ever force him to remain married to me when it had only been an excuse to cancel his wedding.

With a heavy sigh, I hurried to clean up and get ready, doing my best to put this incident behind me. The last thing I wanted was to make things weird between us.

Chapter 6

Rhys

I ALMOST WONDERED IF I had woken up in a mirror universe where everything was the opposite of my normal reality. How else could I explain why the thought of being with Luci aroused me, but being with my fiancée seemed like a fate worse than death?

Back in high school, faking amorous noises while a friend was on a phone call was a fun game we played to mess with our girlfriends. The whole point was to be over-the-top to embarrass each other. It was something stupid that only hormonal boys found amusing. Thus, when Olivia called us cocksuckers, it brought out the immature side of me that decided that would be a great idea.

My goal had been to anger her, but everything muddled in my head as Luci watched. His gaze seared me with heat, devouring me with a dark hunger that lit a fire deep within me. It triggered memories of our drunken caresses after our wedding, pushing my arousal higher. I had been too far gone to prevent myself from wishing he'd take over for real or realizing how weird that desire was.

When Luci ordered me to come, his voice a domineering rumble, my climax almost wasn't fake. It had been hot as fuck hearing him be so authoritative. It filled me with a disconcerting urge for him to pin me down as he dominated my desires, in a way I never knew appealed to me before. I joked about it afterward, but as soon as I was alone in the bathroom, I fantasized about him getting me off as I came for a second time that day because of him. It left me with an uncomfortable ache and a hell of a lot of confusion over what I wanted.

It made me reflect on when we'd practiced kissing each other to prepare for being with girls as teenagers. I had enjoyed it, but I assumed that was kissing in general. Our experimenting with mutual hand jobs had been a natural extension of that. However, before I could kiss him at the same time, his sister had interrupted and ruined everything.

The incident became the thing we never talked about again, which hurt, because I could tell Luci everything—except that I wanted to do it again. How could I say that when he had been so freaked-out over it? It was easier to pretend that it had never happened so that our friendship could stay the same.

But when we had been drinking in bed after my bachelor party, those long-suppressed memories came to the surface. I assumed Luci objected to being with me because we were guys. However, that wasn't the impression I got when I brought it up for the first time since we were teens.

When I propositioned him for a mutual hand job the

night before, his protest had been that he feared Olivia would never let him see me again. He said we couldn't do anything that night because *I* might regret it—not that *we* would. Did that mean he actually wanted that? What if the whole time he considered it "wrong" because we were "just" friends? What if he wanted more but assumed I didn't? More importantly, did I really want that?

On the limo ride to our hotel, we certainly hadn't kissed like it disgusted us. Despite the hangover from hell, waking up naked next to Luci had made me hard—even after I recognized it was him and not Olivia. I *definitely* hadn't imagined him checking out my ass, either. It was an undeniable fact we both got turned on by my aural sex performance, then gotten off on it afterward. The problem was I didn't know what any of that meant.

I required an outside perspective, which was why I brought us back to the Grand Chapel of Graceland. It concerned me how withdrawn Luci had become. After walking up the steps, I paused. "What's wrong?"

He had that furrowed wrinkle between his eyebrows he always got when he worried about something too much. His gaze didn't quite meet mine. "This wasn't where I thought we were going."

"It's the best place for information."

Luci's voice was flat as he pointed out, "We could have looked up how to get an annulment on the internet."

"That's not why we're here."

He startled. "It's not?"

"Nope, we're here for evidence."

Ever the gentleman, Luci held the door for me. "Evidence? For what?"

Before I answered, the woman at the front desk greeted us. "Welcome to the Grand Chapel of Graceland!" She was wearing a bright smile and the ugliest orange taffeta bridesmaid dress in the world. "Hi, I'm Kordaellah."

"Thanks, how's it going?" I returned, walking up to her reception counter.

"It's a sunshine and rainbows kind of day, darling!" She giggled as she beamed at us. "What can I do to make your dreams come true today?"

Her reaction was so saccharine that it should have been cheesy, but her genuine nature charmed me. It drew out my playful side, so I wrapped an arm around Luci's waist and tugged him closer. "We got married here last night and wanted to pick up our photos and certificate."

"Congratulations, that's wonderful!"

"It is, isn't it?"

Luci cleared his throat. "It does seem like a dream."

"Aren't you two sweet?" she cooed. "I'd be happy to help you out with that. What are your names?"

"Lucien St. Amour and Leopold Huntington," he told her.

While she pulled up our info, I joked with Luci, "I always feel like I'm in trouble when you use my full name."

"Right, because you're in trouble with me so often," he sarcastically scoffed.

Kordaellah grinned at him. "I take it he's got you wrapped around his little finger?"

"Since we were toddlers," he retorted. It was funny because it was true.

"Don't feel bad, hon. I wouldn't be able to get mad at his pretty face, either." She gestured for us to follow her. "I'll get you settled in one of our rooms where you can wait while I gather everything for you."

We thanked her as she left us alone in a small conference room, where we sat beside each other at the table that dominated the space. I nudged Luci with my knee to get his attention. "Are you saying I have you whipped already?"

"Name one friend of ours who hasn't said that about me regarding you."

"Come to think of it, you always just rolled your eyes and changed the subject instead of deny it," I realized. "Why's that?"

"Because not a single person would believe me if I denied it," he answered with a huff.

"Does that bother you?"

He shrugged as he adjusted his glasses. "Not really. The only person's opinion I've ever worried about was yours."

I gave him my most charming smile. "I won't complain if you let me get away with murder because of my pretty face."

"It's your damn eyes." His cheeks flushed at his admission.

I rested my chin on my palm, batting my eyelashes at

him. With a heavy Southern drawl, I teased, "Why, Mr. St. Amour, I had no idea you felt that way."

"How is this news to you?" Luci asked with an amused look over my antics.

Kordaellah knocked on the door before entering with an armful of stuff. "Sorry that took so long, boys."

"No problem, we're not in any hurry." I wasn't in a rush to return to the hotel where Olivia was probably lying in wait.

She sat down, then pushed over a black leather book embossed with "Our Wedding" on the front in gold foil. "This is your wedding album that was part of your VIP package. If there are any photos you want in different sizes, we can take care of that for you at cost."

"Can we look at it?" I asked.

"Yes, please! I think you'll be happy. There are some wonderful shots of the two of you together."

I reached out and pulled the album closer, opening it up with a creak of the leather spine. The first picture was a close-up of Luci's hand on top of mine, showing off both our wedding rings. It was another reminder that this was something that we had really done.

The next one was Luci standing at the altar of a beautiful white chapel with a curtain of crystal strands hanging down the walls. He grinned, looking handsome as hell in a black tux with a white rose and blue-purple dendrobium orchid boutonnière. An Elvis impersonator stood nearby wearing a flashy silver jumpsuit. My gaze shifted to the opposite page. It was me laughing as I strutted down the aisle in a white tux, my bouquet matching Luci's lapel flowers.

Luci continued onward. We had giddy smiles as we gazed at each other in the photo. One was of us facing the Elvis minister, holding hands, our fingers interlaced. It was odd, because while I remembered it now, it also was like watching it happen to someone else.

The following two pictures were us putting our rings on each other. It struck me how happy we both appeared. Those weren't the faces of two people who were making a terrible mistake; those were the expressions of two lovers getting married on the happiest day of their lives.

I trembled as I turned the page. My breathing hitched when I saw us kissing after being pronounced husbands. I flushed as I remembered how good it felt to kiss him. If his expression was any indication, he had enjoyed it just as much as me.

The shot on the opposing page twisted my heart in a vice. We rested our foreheads together with our eyes closed, our noses touching, holding hands with serenely happy smiles.

"That one might be my favorite," Kordaellah commented. "It's wonderful to see two people that in love."

I couldn't believe that it was really us. I glanced over at Luci, who was still staring down at the picture with a stunned expression. Whether that was a good thing or a bad thing was hard to tell. "It's beautiful."

"Yeah," he softly agreed.

As we continued, I gasped at the sight of Luci raising

my hand up to press his lips against my wedding band. My smile was happier than I could ever remember feeling before. My heart had fluttered then, the same as it did now. It flustered me how intense Luci's blue eyes were as he looked down at me with absolute adoration. It was suddenly too hot in the small room.

In the next photo, we walked away from the altar. I hugged Luci's arm, resting my head on his shoulder. I radiated joy as he kissed my temple with the utmost tenderness and a pleased smile. There wasn't a shadow of regret or doubt in our expressions; there was only endless excitement.

I wanted to study it longer, but I forced myself to keep going. The following shot was of us walking up the aisle holding hands with a laugh. I grinned, because we both looked like we were having the best time ever. Despite the consequences, it had been fun.

Entertained by our amusement, I hadn't expected the hard punch to the gut awaiting us. We sat on a chapel pew, with Luci's right arm stretched behind me. I nestled against him, intertwining my fingers with his on my shoulder. My bouquet was in my lap as we looked at each other like nothing else mattered other than being together. It was obvious how much I adored my best friend—my *husband*—and that he reciprocated with equal affection. Luci gazed at me as if he loved me with every fiber of his existence and then some.

"This is my favorite." I started getting choked up from the intense rush of feelings. Not once in my life had I felt as beloved as I did in that moment.

"Mine, too," Luci murmured, but I didn't dare look at him when I was so raw and on edge from the revelations.

The last page featured us making out in the limo with "Just Married" written on the back window. I didn't understand any of this. For something that should have been fake, there had been a lot of real love in those photos.

Luci praised Kordaellah. "You guys did a wonderful job."

Thank god he took over, because I couldn't talk. I was too busy trying to figure out what I should do with these intense feelings I had discovered.

"Oh, I knew you'd love them!" she squealed with delight. "As I mentioned earlier, if you're interested in ordering any prints, we can ship them to you later."

"That would be great," he replied.

She passed over a black portfolio. "This is your souvenir marriage certificate. The real one is available in about ten days, so we'll mail that to you, since you'll be on your honeymoon by then."

Fuck, *the honeymoon*. I had completely forgotten about it. Although we were staying in the honeymoon suite at the hotel, I hadn't connected the dots yet. What was I supposed to do about that?

Luci opened it to reveal an ornate certificate. It made our marriage seem more official, despite it not being legally binding. He studied it before saying, "It looks like a diploma, doesn't it?"

The comment was so absurd that I laughed. Finally

finding my voice, I retorted, "I guess that's what you get when you graduate from the single life."

Kordaellah cracked up with peals of laughter, while Luci chuckled at my reaction.

When I worked up the nerve to glance at him, he gave me a reassuring smile. Somehow, everything would be okay. Thank god, because I had no earthly clue what to do about the mess we'd found ourselves in.

"Oh, you boys are too funny." Kordaellah slid a piece of paper over. "I need you to sign this stating that you've received the album and certificate. After that, you're free to head out."

Luci signed it before giving it to me.

I scribbled my signature on it without thought, then returned it to her.

"Still not used to that, huh?" She laughed as she pulled out another sheet. "Don't worry, it happens all the time, so I always print a second copy."

The comment mystified me. "Used to what?"

"Signing with your new name." She gave me the new form. "You've been signing your name one way your whole life, so it takes a while before it feels natural."

"My new name?" I stared in stunned disbelief at the words "Leopold Bertram St. Amour" under the line I had signed as Leopold Bertram Huntington, III.

Kordaellah grinned with a dreamy sigh. "St. Amour is such a romantic name. It fits you both."

Everything screeched to a halt as I realized not only had I married my best friend, but I had taken his last name. I mumbled Luci's name as the revelation overwhelmed me. What had I done?

In tune with my emotions, he requested, "I'm sorry, could you give us a moment?"

"Sure! I'll be up front if you need anything. Take your time, there's no rush."

I didn't even notice she left. All I could focus on was the fact my name was Leopold St. Amour now. Shit, my father would disown me over this.

Luci clasped my shoulder, trying to get my attention. "It's okay, Rhys. We can fix this."

"No!" I exclaimed, the vehemence stunning us both.

"No, what?" His thumb brushed against my collarbone, sending a shiver through me.

I struggled to stay in control of my emotions. "Do you realize what this means?"

"It'll mean a little extra paperwork to change it, but it's fine," he reassured me. "Don't worry, we'll have it changed back before your dad finds out."

"No!" Tears welled up in my eyes as I stared at Luci. I needed him to understand. "It means you've given me the one thing I never thought I could have."

Still looking concerned, he asked, "What's that?"

"I'm not a Huntington anymore." After a lifetime of hating being Huntington the Third, I was free of all the bullshit that name brought me. I was a *St. Amour* now, part of a family that had accepted me, even when my own didn't.

As a tear fell from my eye from the enormity of my situation, Luci brushed it away with such tenderness that it broke me. I clung to him, hiding my face against his neck as a sob escaped me. After the insanity of the morning, the revealing wedding pictures, and finding out that I had a new name, it was too much to bear. I let my tears fall while Luci stroked my back. They wouldn't stop as I sobbed over all the years I'd wasted trying to love the wrong women. More than anything, I cried from the overwhelming relief that he had saved me from making the dumbest decision of my life.

"I'm so sorry," I whispered. It was an inadequate apology for embarrassing myself in front of him again. It was yet another thing I intended to blame my hangover for.

Luci shushed my fears, but he never let go as I tried to regain my composure.

When I pulled away, he wiped the tear streaks from my cheeks. I started to apologize again, but he silenced me by leaning forward and placing a lingering kiss on my forehead. He suggested, "Let's go back to our room."

That he called it "our" room almost made me cry again in my emotional state. I continued fighting back tears as I signed the form with my new name and a flourish.

We didn't say a word as we held hands to leave, carrying the evidence of our marriage that had shown me way more than I'd bargained for.

Chapter 7

Luci

As soon as we returned to the honeymoon suite, Rhys collapsed face-first onto the bed. His outburst in the chapel conference room caught me off guard when I was already unbalanced by my own reactions to the album photographs. We looked like a couple in love with each other, rather than two inebriated best friends who'd eloped on a whim.

It was unnerving seeing the hidden parts of my heart on full display as I gazed at Rhys with feelings I'd convinced myself for years I didn't have. But the most shocking thing had been that he had been looking back at me with love and adoration. How was that possible?

I had spent so long denying that I could have those kinds of emotions for him that it never occurred to me he might feel the same way. Despite having countless girlfriends in the past, neither of us had found true love with any of them. Was this why? Had I been unable to because I loved my best friend without knowing it? It shouldn't have been possible, but it had a ring of truth in it that hurt.

Now that I had incontrovertible proof of how I felt

about Rhys when I let my guard down, how could I go back to only being friends with him? How would I laugh this off as a drunken Vegas mishap that didn't matter? How could I get an annulment when I had real feelings for him?

They were questions without easy answers, so I concentrated on the immediate issue. He was so small on the enormous bed that it brought out my desire to make things better for him.

I got water out of the fridge before sitting next to him. "You should drink."

"I'm never drinking again," he grumbled into the covers.

After such an eventful day, I shared the sentiment, but I tapped the cold bottle against his forehead. "I meant drink water."

Rhys rolled over with a sigh to sit up straight. He gulped down half of it before he asked with a wry grin, "Don't you ever tire of taking care of me?"

I should have cracked a joke about it, but I answered, "No."

"I'm a fucking mess, Luci." He picked at the label. "How are you not sick of me?"

"It's been a batshit insane day. After the amount of what-the-fucks we've dealt with today, you're doing fine."

He snorted at that. "I don't think weeping is doing fine."

"That was about more than this. It was years of shit coming to a head."

"How do you always know?" Rhys's stormy gray eyes

begged me for answers. "How do you understand me better than myself sometimes?"

"You're not as complicated as you think."

Still messing with the bottle, he requested, "I know we have to talk about everything, but can we take a nap? I'm fucking exhausted."

"Sure." I stood up to go, but Rhys grabbed my wrist to stop me.

"Don't leave." He tightened his grip on me. "This bed is the size of an ocean, so it won't be weird. Please stay?"

How could I say no when he stared up at me with such a vulnerable expression in his gray-blue eyes? "Okay, but are you sure you don't want lunch, though? It would help."

"We can order room service after." He held on to me as if he feared I would change my mind and leave him.

"Sounds good, although you have to let go of me."

He jerked his hand away. "Sorry."

"It's okay."

I started unbuttoning my shirt out of habit as I walked to the other side but stopped when I realized it might be uncomfortable for Rhys under the circumstances. Before I could ask if it was a problem, he stripped down to his briefs and got into bed. "Well, I guess that answers that question."

Realization dawned on him at what he had done. "Sorry, I can get dressed if—"

He cut himself off when I shrugged off my shirt to drop onto the floor and stripped off my pants before I did the same. I put my glasses on the nightstand before settling. My exhaustion overtook me as I relaxed. It had been one hell of a day considering it wasn't even noon yet.

However, no matter how bone-weary tired I was, my mind raced too fast to fall asleep. My thoughts centered on what we would do about our marriage and our recently discovered feelings for each other. That meant figuring out what I wanted. Did I want Rhys that way? Could he want me like that? It was crazy, right? Or was it?

I heard him rustling in the sheets. It surprised me, because he normally fell asleep before his head even hit the pillow. I envied that about him, since I had problems getting to sleep thanks to my dumbass brain that liked to overthink everything.

Rhys's reaction to his new last name troubled me. He had a difficult relationship with his parents through no fault of his own. They came from old money, so his father acted as if that made them superior to everyone else. He had expected his son to follow in his footsteps and work at their multibillion-dollar real estate enterprise, despite treating him with contempt his whole life. Nothing Rhys did was ever good enough, so at some point he'd stopped trying. After he defied Leo by starting his own tech firm instead of going into the family business, they had quit speaking to each other. The saddest part was it had improved things between them.

When he was a kid, Rhys's mother let the nannies raise him. There was a modicum of kindness in Lydia, but she was as obsessed with their family worth as her husband. I couldn't think of a single occasion when she'd stood up for him against his unreasonable father. She hadn't written Rhys out of her life when Leo did, but her reaction at breakfast didn't bode well for the future.

I never understood why the two people who should love him the most didn't. All he wanted was their affection, which they were incapable of giving him. They were the most selfish and self-absorbed parents I knew, who only cared that he wasn't embarrassing them. Given the spectacle we'd made at breakfast, I could only imagine what hell he was in for later.

Because of his strained relationship at home, Rhys spent as much time at my house as possible. My family loved him like he was my actual brother. We joked that he was an honorary St. Amour, but now he was one for real. That's when it hit me—I had been so fixated on Rhys's family that I completely forgot we hadn't told mine yet.

"Are you awake?"

I turned to glance over at him. His face pinched with worry again. "I am, but why are you?"

"Luci, your family," he said in a panicked voice, surprising me that his thoughts paralleled my own. His breathing quickened. "Fuck, I've ruined everything. They'll hate me and—"

I felt ridiculous having this kind of conversation with so much distance between us, so I scooted closer to him. "You need to quit jumping to the worst-case scenario."

"Your mom and sister are going to be upset that we got married without them, not to mention that we did it for the wrong reasons. Your dad is going to be so disappointed in me." Rhys groaned into the pillow. "I can't lose them. They're all I have now, because I'm getting disowned after this morning at breakfast and changing my name."

"They love you too much for that to happen," I reminded him. "Once they get over the shock, everyone will celebrate you going from an honorary member of our family to an official one."

Rhys remained silent as he hid his face from me, but I saw him trembling.

"What are you really worried about?"

I waited for him to find the courage to say whatever was on his mind. It took a while for him to confess in an anguished whisper, "Even if we have to annul this, I don't want to be a Huntington again."

My foolish heart cheered that he hadn't insisted that we needed to dissolve our marriage. I hesitated before I reached out and placed my hand on his back to reassure him. "You don't have to."

"Really?" He looked at me with guarded hope.

"You've always been a part of our family. Now, you have the paperwork to prove it. I won't take that from you if you decide to get an annulment."

He startled me when he threw himself on me in an awkward hug again. "Thank you."

Without meaning to, I stroked his hair in silent comfort. "Besides, I'm glad you did it."

"Changed my name?"

"Yeah, because being a Huntington has brought you

nothing but problems and pain. At least as a St. Amour, you know you'll always have love watching over you."

Rhys swore with a laugh, "Goddamn it, you're going to make me cry again."

"Sorry." My sentimentality embarrassed me, but it was true.

He snuggled closer. "Can I stay here?"

"As long as you want." The words had a much deeper meaning now.

Rhys relaxed into my embrace with a soft sigh. It felt so right to hold him in my arms I never wanted to let him go. Rather than overthinking it, I focused on enjoying hugging him.

I grinned when he succumbed to sleep in record time. With the reassuring weight of him on me, it didn't take long before I joined him.

Chapter 8

Rhys

To keep my mind off Luci in the shower, I summoned my personal assistant, Xander Dandridge. He was a handsome guy with striking green-hazel eyes, who had worked for me for almost five years. Thanks to his delicate features and kind heart, he was the heartthrob of my office. He was in Vegas to be a guest at my wedding, so I regretted having to call on him for help when he was supposed to be on vacation. However, I knew if I wanted something done right, he was the man to take care of things. I'd apologize with a nice bonus for him when I got back.

As we sat in the hotel suite living room, I briefed him on the details of my recent nuptials. I then requested his help with something that had been weighing on me since our visit to the chapel. "I need you to change my honeymoon bookings at the Luxurian Suites Resort for Luci to join me. If you have to cancel the flights and rebook them under our names instead, that's fine. Do whatever you have to do so I don't run into Olivia in Greece while I'm there with him. I don't care what it costs." I should have asked Luci first, but forgiveness was easier than permission.

"Sure, I'll take care of it," Xander promised. "Do I need to have someone get Lucien's passport from home and deliver it here?"

"No, he doesn't have a driver's license, so he uses his passport for ID at the airport, even for domestic flights," I told him.

"Great, I'll also start canceling the wedding bookings. With such short notice, most of it will be nonrefundable, but—"

I waved his concern away. "I'm fine with paying for the privilege to *not* be married to Olivia."

"Understood."

"Honestly, the only reason I feel bad canceling is because all the time you spent coordinating with the wedding planner will go to waste. I'm sorry, Xander. I promise I'll make it up to you when I return from our honeymoon."

"That's very kind of you but unnecessary. Thank you."

"Well, that and we won't be able to enjoy that incredible wedding cake we picked out." I pouted at that. Olivia had refused to sample cake because of the calories, so Luci had gone with me to all the bakeries for tastings. It had been so much fun, not to mention delicious. "Damn, that was the only part of the wedding I was looking forward to."

He made me laugh when he asked, "You mean other than it finally being over?"

"Yeah, you're right about that. Oh, speaking of finally being over, that reminds me. Have a locksmith change all the locks at my house as soon as possible. I don't want Olivia in my place while I'm gone."

"If you're comfortable with my friend Jules being there to handle it in person, I can have someone over in a few hours," he offered.

"She's your friend, so that's cool with me." Anybody he would vouch for would be trustworthy.

He grinned wryly. "Jules is a guy."

When he said that, I remembered who he was referring to. "He's your friend that comes to the office for lunch sometimes, right?"

"Yep, that would be him."

I had talked to Jules on numerous occasions over the years, so there was no excuse for my mistake. "Sorry, it's been a hell of a day. I'd really appreciate it if Jules would take care of that for me. Of course, I'll make sure he's properly compensated for his time." The irony of my mistake wasn't lost on me. "Wow, as often as people think Luci is my girlfriend because of his nickname, you'd think I would be more sensitive to that issue."

"No worries."

It made me realize, "Huh, people will probably assume Luci's my wife now." What would he think of that? I suppose it depended on if we stayed in the marriage or not.

"Permission to speak freely, sir?"

When Xander had first started working for me, I had tried to stop him from referring to me as "sir." It seemed ridiculous when we were so close in age, but he preferred that level of professionalism. I allowed it since it didn't bother me enough to make it an issue. He had no problem speaking his mind, so his request for permission was unusual. "Sure."

"For what it's worth, I'm glad you married Lucien instead of Olivia."

I arched an eyebrow. "Why's that?"

"Because you actually love each other." It was undeniable, but it surprised me to hear him state it with such conviction. Then again, he was one of the closest people to me. "You deserve that instead of someone who was only chasing after you for your fortune. Now, you can be happy."

My gaze drifted to the closed bedroom door, where Luci was showering. The thought of him wet and naked in the enormous shower filled me with an unfamiliar heat, but I did my best to ignore it. That wasn't a fantasy I should explore while someone was still in the room with me. I forced my attention back to my assistant. "I sure hope so."

"Congratulations, Rhys." He stood up to leave. "Once I finish with everything, I'll send you an email confirming it."

"Sounds great, thanks."

When Xander opened the door, Ambrose and August were standing on the other side of it. Ambrose entered with a slight smirk, wearing a black button-down shirt that revealed his smooth chest and showed off his bulging muscles. His auburn hair, blue eyes, handsome face, and Irish brogue meant he never had any shortage of women. "You're already bored with Lucien and moving on to someone younger? You sure don't waste any time, do you, Rhys?"

I rolled my eyes, while Xander arched an elegant eyebrow. As much as I didn't want to deal with Ambrose's good-natured ribbing, it was a welcome distraction from what Luci was doing behind the bedroom door. "No, he's my personal assistant."

"Is that what you're calling it now?" Ambrose asked, laying his Irish accent on thick for Xander's sake. While he was heterosexual, he wasn't above flirting with attractive men to stroke his ego. He blatantly checked out Xander from head to toe and back again. Whenever he did things like that, Luci's theory that Ambrose was trying too hard to be straight made a lot of sense. "He's cute, I'll give you that."

"If you'll excuse me," Xander primly said before brushing past them to attend to my business.

Ambrose took it as permission to come over to the living room area, sitting in my employee's vacated seat. "Where's your blushing bride?"

August sat beside him on the love seat with a sigh. He looked aggrieved over more than just that comment. It made me wonder if they'd had a recent fight. "You know that's offensive, right?"

Poor August. He always got stuck trying to rein in Ambrose's smart mouth. The two of them side by side were quite the sight. Ambrose's massive body dwarfed August's slight build. While Ambrose was considered handsome by most, August's high cheekbones and green eyes made him fall more on the pretty side of the good-looking spectrum. Always fashionably dressed, he managed to pull off a pompadour hairstyle that would have looked ridiculous on most men. He looked amazing as ever in his well-tailored purple blazer over a pink shirt paired with skintight white jeans.

As odd as their friendship seemed from the outside, they balanced each other out somehow. Ambrose helped August come out of his shell, while August kept Ambrose from going overboard with his "too much gene" propensity for being extra. It was a classic case of opposites attract, only they were just friends. Luci had suspected since college that August harbored secret feelings for Ambrose, but I found it hard to believe given their many girlfriends. Then again, the same was true for me, and now I had a husband. Would that ever stop being weird?

I rejoined the conversation when Ambrose continued, "Congrats on making it official."

"Making it official?"

"Yeah. I mean, it's obvious you two have been a thing for years."

That was news to me. "Is that so?"

"I'm thrilled for you," August added. "It's great you don't have to hide it anymore."

"We weren't hiding anything," I defend myself. "It's not like we've been together this whole time. I wasn't cheating on Olivia with him."

"It was more like you were cheating on him with her," Ambrose said. August elbowed him with a look over the insensitive comment. "I'm not saying you were. But any idiot could see you love Lucien a hell of a lot more than her."

I shrugged. "I guess that makes me the biggest idiot of all." Thankfully, I had noticed before it was too late. This was my opportunity to clear up the misunderstanding with my friends and explain the marriage was an impulsive mistake, but the words wouldn't come. How could I call it a mistake when it had been the best decision I had ever made? The wedding photos were incontrovertible proof of the love between us. We just needed to be brave enough to embrace it. Going on the honeymoon together would give us the chance to try.

"Yeah, you're an idiot to let a woman as gorgeous as Olivia get away." Ambrose gave me a charming smile. "I don't suppose you'd mind if I consoled her after she was so cruelly jilted right before her wedding?"

"Haven't you tortured Katie enough?" It surprised me to hear August sticking up for her. "You've already broken her heart. Don't shatter it further by nailing her sister."

The flare of August's possessive jealousy would only add to Luci's conviction that there was something more between them. I wasn't sure if it was true or not, but I figured it wouldn't hurt to help August in case it was. "Don't bother. I promise you Olivia's not worth it."

"But you still intended to marry her?" Ambrose asked in surprise.

"I was doing what I thought I was supposed to do," I

explained. "But I realized doing what I wanted to do was the smarter decision."

Ambrose's lips curved upward into a perverse grin. "And you wanted to do Lucien."

If my hard-on and jerking off to a fantasy of Luci twice that morning was any indication, I apparently wanted that very much. While I still didn't know if that was what I was after, at least one part of me had no reservations. I settled for wolfishly grinning as an answer.

Luci emerged from the bedroom, wearing nothing but a towel and holding his phone. My heart stuttered in my chest as I drank in the sight of his glistening skin, his rock-hard abs, and the white fabric hanging perilously low on his hips. He was dripping with sex, setting me afire with lust. My dick was in favor of throwing our friends out and seeing what was under that towel. I got further distracted by a droplet of water falling from his hair, sliding down to his collarbone. I wanted to lick it off, then kiss the tiny mole on his neck and the one above his hip.

"Rhys, is that a yes?"

At the sound of my name, my gaze snapped up to Luci's. He was looking at me expectantly. I had clearly missed whatever it was he had asked me. "Uh..."

He repeated himself. "My parents want to move dinner up to six o'clock. Is that okay with you?"

It was hard to look away from his perfection, but I checked the time on my watch. It was almost five thirty. "Yeah, I'm okay with it."

"Damn, Lucien. You're putting me to shame,"

Ambrose commented as he gave him a once-over. "Looks like I need to hit the gym more."

Every ridge of Luci's muscles beckoned me to come closer and explore them with my tongue and fingertips. How had I never noticed my best friend was walking sex on legs? And what the hell was I supposed to do with this new lust for him burning inside me?

"You're built enough as it is." August's cheeks flushed as he stared at his hands in his lap. "If you get jacked any further, I bet you could bench-press me with one hand."

"I never turn down a bet." Ambrose chuckled, causing August's blush to deepen. "If you're volunteering, I'd be down to try."

Luci's lips curved upward with a knowing smile. "The gym's on the fifth floor. Have fun, boys. Don't hurt yourselves."

"And that's our cue to leave," August said, standing up to go.

Ambrose grinned as he loomed over his shorter friend, getting in his personal space. "Are you that eager for me to show you how strong I am?"

Based on August's rosy cheeks and inability to look Ambrose in the eyes, the answer to that question was a resounding "yes." *Damn, looks like Luci was right again.*

August reminded Ambrose, "They have dinner at six, remember? We need to go so they can get ready."

"Or squeeze in a quickie before they leave," Ambrose quipped.

His words triggered a mental image of Luci pinning me down, pressing his perfect body against mine as we kissed. It sent a jolt of desire and adrenaline running through me. My cheeks were as pink as August's from the thought. Is that what I wanted? My dick's opinion was a very enthusiastic "hell yeah," but the rest of me wasn't as confident.

"Congratulations, guys. We'll see you after the honeymoon," August said.

Before Ambrose could say something regrettable, August ushered him out of the room, leaving me alone with Luci. I feared he might see straight through to my perverse fantasies, so I got off the couch to walk over to my suitcase.

When Luci captured my wrist to stop me, our bodies collided against each other, sending my hormones haywire. This close, the heat radiated off him from his shower. He liked them on the hottest setting. He once melted the tub sealant of his second-floor bathroom and caused a leak in the first floor's ceiling, baffling the repair guy.

The smell of Luci's body wash was intoxicating. It was a mixture of smoky vanilla and mahogany, with a hint of musk. I responded to it on a primal level that made me want to jump him regardless of how straight I had thought I was. Breathing became a challenge the longer he stared at me with his dark eyes that seared my soul with the desire burning in them.

Being so close was too much temptation to resist. I reached up with my free hand, running over the defined abs that I had been admiring earlier. He inhaled at the unexpected touch as my fingertips traced over the strong planes of his chest. When he didn't reject me, I decided fuck it, why should I start worrying about consequences now? I entangled my fingers in his wet hair at the base of his neck and guided him down for an intense kiss.

Rather than jerking away, Luci pulled me closer. I yielded to his tongue with a moan, letting him take what he wanted from me. I had never been more turned on in my life as we made out. His towel didn't hide how aroused he was as his hardness pressed against me. His grip on my wrist tightened, making me whimper. I ached for him to throw me on the bed and take control of my desires.

When we paused for air, he rested his forehead against mine, overwhelmed by the experience. I was the first to speak when I pleaded, "Tell me we can be late and keep going."

"If we continue, we'll miss dinner," Luci said, his voice a dark rumble that sent shivers through me.

I looked up at him with an impish grin. "Promise?"

"I've waited too long to rush this." The sentiment was simultaneously romantic, depressing, and frustrating as hell. We were so stupid for resisting the pull between us for so long. "Plus, we haven't eaten since yesterday."

"Is that your way of saying I need to keep up my strength for what comes after dinner?"

A shadow of doubt clouded Luci's eyes. "Only if it's what you want."

I guided his hand to my answering hardness as proof. His fingers twitched as he cupped my raging erection.

"Oh, I want it. I've wanted it since that night your sister interrupted us pleasuring each other."

"Rhys." I loved how Luci whispered my name like it was a sacred word.

"Please put on some damn clothes, before I make us miss dinner."

"Only because I have to, not because I want to." With that, he returned to the bathroom to finish getting ready.

Even though we stopped before we reached the good part, I was on cloud nine after that incredible kiss. I couldn't wait until after dinner when we could do something about the feelings we had been dancing around since we were teenagers.

I ALWAYS LOOKED FORWARD to meals with Luci's family, but this was the first time that I was nervous before meeting them. The idea that we might have hurt them by eloping in secret killed me.

Outside of the restaurant, Luci told me, "I'll follow your lead, okay?"

"You say that like I know what I'm doing." I nervously laughed. What if I screwed everything up with his family? I'd have no one after that.

As if he could sense the road my thoughts were going down, he reassured me. "Remember, we're in this together."

His parents and sister were already sitting at a table waiting. My nerves reached a fevered pitch, making me feel sick. My turmoil must have shown on my face, because Luci's mom got up from her chair.

Vera's expression was sympathetic as she opened her arms to me. "Oh, honey, come here."

I stepped into the hug, overcome with emotions. While I didn't deserve her comfort, I clung to her, careful to hide my wedding ring.

"Whatever happened, it's okay," she promised. Her words soothed me, making believe it was true. "You're with family now."

Would she still say that after I told them the truth?

Like the perfect mom she was, Vera didn't pull away. My mother hadn't even looked at me, let alone hug me after my announcement. I hadn't received so much as a text from either of my parents, but that wasn't surprising after the blowout at breakfast.

As soon as I stepped out of Vera's arms, Luci's sister gathered me into a tight hug. "I swear to god, I will kick Olivia's ass for this if you want me to."

I appreciated that Lucretia was fiercely protective of me. Not only was she like a sister to me, but she also was one of my closest friends. I originally wanted her to be one of my groomsmen, but Olivia threw a fit at the idea and refused. "But this is all my fault."

"Nope, it's hers for being awful." She pulled back and grinned at me. I realized she was wearing the emerald-green sweater and purple pants I had given her two Christmases ago. It was yet another indicator of how much Luci's family cared about me. "Thanks for realizing it before you made the biggest mistake of your life."

I couldn't share her humor. "I'm sorry I'm such an idiot."

"That doesn't stop me from loving my brother, and it's never stopped me from loving you," Lucretia teased. "You know that."

"Yeah, but—"

She shushed me. "You're fine, Rhys."

"Mighty, mighty fine, actually," I retorted, causing her to laugh. It was our long-running joke.

"No argument there, hon." She winked at me, before she hugged Luci. I heard her whisper to him, "Good job." It was zero percent surprising that Lucretia had figured out that whatever made me call off my engagement was because of him. I was apparently the only moron who hadn't realized that my entire life revolved around him.

Luci's dad came over to me next. The family resemblance was strong between father and son. Luke was a preview of the handsome silver fox his son would be someday. He wore a dark blue sweater with a white shirt collar under it paired with jeans.

I admired and respected Luke more than anyone in my family. From my earliest memories, Luke and the entire St. Amour family treated me like a second son. Without question, he gave me the love and approval my dad was incapable of giving me. I could live with my asshole father hating me for the rest of my life, but not Luke. For the first time since I was fifteen and accidentally broke his car window, I stared up at him with fear of reprisal.

Luke clasped me on the shoulder with a gentle

squeeze. "You look too miserable for a man who made the right decision, son."

He always called me "son," but the word hit me hard in my emotional state. "But everyone tried to warn me." My throat closed up from my overwhelming emotions. "I'm so sorry, I should have—"

Luke stopped me with a hug and a reassuring pat on the back. "No apologies are necessary. The only thing we care about is that you're happy."

"I am."

"That's all that matters. Let's get you something to eat."

With that, we all took our seats. Luke sat at the head, with Vera and Lucretia on one side, me and Luci on the other. The normalcy of seating arrangement helped soothe my nerves, as did Luci giving my hand a reassuring squeeze under the table.

Once we placed our orders, Lucretia asked, "Am I allowed to guess why you called off the wedding?"

"Besides the obvious reason she was all wrong for him?" Vera countered, grinning. She was honest to a fault, but I loved that about her.

"Something else happened. Let me think." Lucretia tapped her chin as she considered her options. After a moment, her smile turned mischievous. "They eloped!"

I stared at Luci in disbelief. "You told them?"

"*What?*" Lucretia screeched, drawing looks from other people at nearby tables. We really needed to quit making a scene in restaurants.

"No, you just did," he said under his breath.

My eyes went wide, realizing I had inadvertently fessed up to what we had done. I froze like a deer caught in headlights, uncertain of what to do. That wasn't the way I wanted them to find out.

To my great shock, the two women began laughing hysterically. Luke grinned as they wiped away the tears of mirth gathering in the corners of their eyes. That wasn't the type of crying I had expected from them.

Once Lucretia regained her composure, she held her palm out to her parents. It was reminiscent of Luci demanding the honeymoon suite key card at breakfast. "Pay up, folks. You each owe me a hundred bucks."

"You placed bets?" Luci questioned in a scandalized tone.

His sister sounded downright gleeful. "I had money on you two eloping. Mom bet on Olivia getting caught having an affair with Ambrose. Dad thought Rhys would go through with it."

Their wagers probably should have offended me, but as I watched Vera and Luke pull out their wallets to pay their daughter, the absurdity of it struck me. It was my turn to be the one laughing. It was such a St. Amour thing to do I couldn't help but be in awe of it.

Lucretia pocketed her windfall, then blew me a kiss with a wink. "Thanks, hon."

"You're not mad?" Luci asked.

With a dramatic sigh, Vera joked, "We all know I'd lose that money playing slots later. It's fine."

Luci frowned. "I meant about us getting married."

"I'll only be mad if there aren't pictures," Lucretia answered. "I want to see your rings!"

When he showed he was wearing Olivia's ostentatious wedding band, she cackled again with peals of laughter. "Oh, you didn't just steal her man, you stole her ring, too? Beautifully done, Luci!"

"And her honeymoon suite," he added.

The information delighted Lucretia. "You're such a petty bastard! Serves her right."

I justified our actions. "It's not that we didn't want you there. It was a spur-of-the-moment idea and—"

Vera interrupted me. "We'll forgive you if we can throw you a proper wedding later."

"We couldn't be prouder to have you as an official member of the St. Amour family, son." Luke smiled at me with so much fatherly pride that I could have cried again.

It was my last chance to explain there would be an annulment and not a second wedding, but I couldn't bring myself to say it. Everything in my head was a jumbled mess, but I knew in my heart that I wasn't ready to give up Luci.

"Please tell me there was an Elvis impersonator involved!" Lucretia begged.

"It's Vegas. There's always an Elvis," I said with a laugh. "The chapel e-mailed me an online photo album earlier."

Lucretia did a happy clap as she bounced in her chair. "I love show-and-tell!"

I hesitated before agreeing. Our open affection in the pictures was a very personal thing to share. I glanced over at Luci, who nodded at me. With his consent, I pulled up the gallery before handing over my phone.

As Lucretia and Vera cooed over the photos, I interlaced my fingers with Luci's. The small gesture made him smile in a way that sent love blooming anew in my heart. No matter what happened, as long as I had him at my side, everything would be okay. In that regard, absolutely nothing had changed between us.

Chapter 9

Luci

As relieved as I was that my family had taken the news of the marriage well, their enthusiastic excitement made me feel hollow. None of this was real. I waited the whole dinner for Rhys to mention the annulment, but it never happened. I told myself not to read too much into it. My foolish heart wished it was because he didn't want it anymore, but the more likely case was he probably wanted to avoid upsetting everyone with the truth.

When we returned to our honeymoon suite, I decided it was time for answers. I stopped him in the living room, standing closer than was necessary. As I looked down into his wide stormy gray eyes, it was hard not to get lost in them.

Decades of our friendship had taught me that being blunt was the best way to handle Rhys. "Why didn't you tell them about the annulment?"

His eyes were full of challenge as he declared, "I don't want to."

The rebellion was as infuriating as it was invigorating. I tipped his chin back, holding his gaze as used my height to my advantage to press closer to him. "Why don't you want to tell me?"

"No, I don't want to get an annulment."

For such a simple sentence, it baffled me. I told myself not to get my hopes up when he only meant he didn't want one right now. Later would be a different story. "What do you mean?"

A grin tugged at the corner of Rhys's mouth. "You're supposed to be the smart one. If you can't figure it out—"

"Don't play games with me, Rhys," I sharply interrupted him. I softened my tone when I saw him wince at my words. "Not about this."

Defiance burned bright in his eyes, sending a twisted thrill through me. "Fine, I'll explain since you apparently require it to be explicitly spelled out for you. I want you to kiss me until I forget how to breathe. I want you to take me into our bedroom right now and finish what we started that night as teenagers and keep going. I want to go on our honeymoon together and have you pound me into the mattress until I'm hoarse from crying out your name. Then, I want you to make love to me until your name is the only word I remember. I want to come home with you afterward and see where this goes." Rhys reached up and caressed my cheek as I stared at him in shock. "I want to be your husband for real, Lucien."

For once in my life, I was speechless. My emotions were a confusing jumble of being turned on by his vivid descriptions of how he wanted me to pleasure him and being overwhelmed by his unwavering certainty. It was everything I desired, but I feared the best thing that had ever happened to me would disappear. "But this morning—"

"This morning doesn't count. I can safely say that this has been the longest and most eventful day of my damn life. What I said then doesn't matter. I'm standing in front of you telling you what I want right now." He pulled off his sweater, throwing it aside without a care where it landed. When he stripped off his jeans and underwear at the same time, my brain short-circuited at the sight of his glorious nudity. "What I want right now is for you to get naked so we can find out what happens when your sister can't interrupt us."

I prevented him from undoing the buttons of my shirt. As I held his thin wrists in my hands, I struggled between accepting his offer and protecting myself from hurt when he regretted his decision. "I can't do this and then go back to the way it was before," I warned, tightening my hold on him. "It would break me."

"Well, luckily for us, I have no interest in changing my mind." He implored me with his eyes to believe his sincerity. "I wasn't lying when I said I've wanted this since we were teenagers. I've never had a kiss that made my heart race the same way until I kissed you again today."

It was surreal hearing that Rhys had the same experience I did. I had tried so hard to convince myself it was because it was our first kiss that it differed from the rest. Our kiss before dinner had shown it was so much more than that, though.

I remained silent, but he continued persuading me he was serious. He never looked away as he confessed, "Since I'm being honest, I wanted to try again. But you were so freaked-out after your sister almost caught us, I didn't bring it up again. I was scared I would lose you if I pushed for another chance, so I pretended like nothing happened."

It gutted me knowing that he wished we had tried again. I hated admitting, "I panicked."

"About what?"

It was a deceptively simple question, with a very complicated answer. I had barely been honest with myself about what had happened back then, too scared to confront the overwhelming truth that would have changed our friendship forever. The depths of what I had felt for Rhys during those intimate moments had terrified me so deeply that I desperately pretended everything was a lie until it became true. But now, with nowhere left to run, it was time to own up to what I had avoided for far too long.

Rhys's voice was gentle, like he was coaxing a scared animal. "You can tell me, Lucien."

It was so rare for him to use my full name it did weird things to my heart when he did. If I confessed, there was no taking it back. It would forever be there between us. But I didn't see any other option. Plus, I was delusional if I thought he hadn't figured out what I was hiding. Nobody knew me better than him.

I took a deep breath, then admitted the truth I had ignored for half my life. "I panicked when I realized that

I loved you." When Rhys didn't pull away from me, the words came out in a torrent. "I wanted to be more than friends, but I thought you were only fooling around. If we hooked up again, you'd figure it out and you wouldn't want to be my friend anymore. I couldn't lose you because of a stupid teenage crush."

He stroked my cheek with his thumb, his eyes full of so much understanding as he comforted me, I could have cried. "But it wasn't just a stupid teenage crush, was it?"

I shook my head, unable to respond with words.

"Your sister is right. We're colossal idiots," Rhys said with a rueful sigh. "We both ran away from our feelings because we were so afraid of losing each other."

"It would destroy me." I knew that with absolute certainty.

He shoved my shoulder. "Do you think it wouldn't do the same to me?" His expression turned ornery. "Do you think I was imagining you as 'just a friend' when I was jerking off in the shower this morning?"

In my shock, I couldn't answer him.

"Do you think I believe you were imaging me as 'just a friend' when *you* got off earlier?"

My cheeks flushed at the question.

Rhys continued. "Do you have any idea how much it turned me on knowing you were getting off thinking about me? How hot it made me when I caught you checking out my ass?"

"But I shouldn't—"

Instead of arguing with me further, he grabbed my

shirt and used it to yank me into an aggressive kiss. I growled as our tongues battled for dominance. It was an extremely effective way to silence all of my protests and fears.

We were breathless when he pulled back for air. His lips were slick and swollen, making me harder and hornier than I had ever been before. He went for my shirt buttons again, but this time I didn't have the willpower to stop him.

He paused to say, "To be clear, I wasn't doing that as 'just a friend.' I did that as your husband. And if you don't hurry and take me—"

That was all I needed to hear. I bent down and scooped him up in a fireman's cradle hold, causing him to yelp in surprise. He wrapped his arms around me to steady himself as I carried him to the bedroom.

"You're carrying me over the threshold? Aren't you a romantic softie." Rhys started trailing distracting kisses up my neck.

"I can assure you, no part of me is soft right now."

Rhys's laughter was light and free, healing my old hurt. I set him down on his feet near the bed. My clothes disappeared as fast as I could strip out of them. I drank in the sight of him, lingering on his hardness jutting out as evidence of how aroused he was.

It was the best kind of dream. I held him close as I claimed his mouth, overly aware of his rigid length pressed against my body. It filled me with an urge to throw him on the bed and ravage him. I settled for letting my hands slide down the curve of his spine and over the gorgeous swell of his ass to grope it.

"Bed. *Now*," Rhys ordered, the authoritative tone sending a shiver through me. When I didn't act fast enough, he shoved me onto it. Before I could reposition myself, he straddled my lap, grinding against me. He kissed me like it was the only thing giving him life. There was nothing in the world that would make me stop him from doing what he wanted when it felt this good.

Unable to resist temptation, I let my fingers slide between his crack and run over his hole. His body thrust back on the sensation, inspiring me with ideas I never would have been bold enough to act on as a teenager.

Before I could do anything else, Rhys pushed me flat on my back. He braced his hands on either side of my head and bent down to kiss me again. I wrapped my arms around him, entangling my fingers in his sandy-blond hair as we devoured each other to make up for lost time. We broke apart with a gasp when he thrust his hardness against mine. He did it again, and a feral noise escaped me.

His hips jerked at the sound. "Fuck, that's so sexy!"

It gave me an idea. "Do you have lotion?"

Instead of answering me, he kissed the mole on my neck with a satisfied murmur. "Mm, I've wanted to do that since you walked out in a towel." He touched the one above my hips. "This one, too."

It was adorable, but I had more pressing needs. "While that's all well and good, what about lotion?"

He grumbled in between pecks along my collarbone, "Are you seriously going to make me go get it?"

"I suppose we could call room service and ask," I drolly retorted.

Rhys muttered something as he slid off me to stumble into the bathroom, giving me a chance to calm myself. It would be unforgivable to come early and put a stop to things when I was finally getting what I wanted. I repositioned myself in the middle of the bed to give us more space to explore.

He returned triumphant, clambering to straddle over me again.

I had expected lotion, but he came prepared with lube. With an arched eyebrow, I asked, "Do I want to know why you have this?"

Rhys squirmed on top of me in a way that made me want to get on with it. "Well, I suppose I could lie and say Olivia was drier than the Gobi Desert, or I could own up to the fact that I'm *really* into ass play."

This time both of my eyebrows raised in surprise. "Is that so?"

His grin was perverse and beautiful. "I figured that many gay men couldn't be wrong, so I started experimenting in college. Turns out I'm super into it."

It was rare for me to learn something about Rhys I didn't already know, so the news astonished me. "But I was your roommate. How did I not know?"

"Because I had the decency to wait until you had lacrosse practice," he said with a laugh.

The mental image of him teasing his hole in our old

dorm room was almost too much for me. "*That's* what you did when I left?"

He snorted at my reaction. "What did you think I did when you weren't there? Homework?"

I shrugged. "Jerked off?"

"Oh, I did that, too." Rhys wrapped his hand around my dick, tempting me with slow strokes. "I'm great at multitasking. But I figured I didn't need to bring my dildo in here when I have you right here and willing. The better question is, what did you have in mind when you asked for a lubricant?"

I sounded uncertain when I admitted, "Jerking us both off at the same time."

"Well, I certainly won't say no to that." He held out his palm. I obliged him by dispensing enough lube for both of us, before capping the bottle and casting it aside.

Just like when we were teens, he didn't hesitate when he reached for my cock. The confident way he worked me made me quiver. How was this real?

I reminded myself I wasn't dreaming when I started working Rhys's member at the same time. He thrust into my fist with a whimper. The dual sensation of touching him while being touched by him was almost more than my brain could process. Between being with Rhys and how long it had been since I had been intimate with someone, I raced toward my climax. I wouldn't last much longer, so I changed things up a bit.

"Move back." I loved that he obeyed without question.

"Like this?"

"Perfect." I took both of us in my large hand to stroke our cocks together.

He scrambled for a hold on my shoulder as he leaned forward. His wanton keens were music to my ears as he rutted against me. "Luci!"

The sound of him calling out my name made me come hard. I gasped as cum spurted onto my stomach from the most satisfying orgasm of my life.

Rhys followed suit, trembling from the intensity of his climax. He collapsed on my chest with a satisfied moan, boneless in his ecstasy and uncaring of the mess between us.

I wiped my hand on the sheet before I embraced him. For the first time since I was a teenager, I was at peace and gratified. We both were adrift in the afterglow of our release.

Eventually, Rhys laughed.

"What's so funny?"

With an effort, he propped himself up to look at me. He answered with amusement, "Shit, no wonder your sister heard all our muffled moaning and came to check if you were having a nightmare. We're noisy as hell."

We shared a laugh. "In other words, you're saying it's a good thing that she's fifteen floors below with a locked door in between us?"

"That, and I'm super glad I don't have to sneak out the window with a boner this time," he retorted. "A shower would be a great, though."

As much as I didn't want to move, the cooling mess on my stomach made a convincing argument for getting clean. Plus, I'd have to be dead to turn down being wet and naked with Rhys.

He smiled at me, and in that moment, I knew I was his forever. I always had been. I couldn't help but think it had been worth the wait to call him mine.

Chapter 10

Rhys

Our fourteen-hour trip to Mykonos, Greece, ended up taking almost nineteen due to delays. By the time we reached the Luxurian Suites Resort, we passed out the minute we arrived. It wasn't quite the way I had imagined the first night of my honeymoon going.

The softest of caresses woke me up the next day. It drew my attention to the fact that Luci was spooning me from behind, his hardness pressing against me as he trailed his fingers over my skin. I shivered with lust, my cock perking up with interest. A breathy whimper escaped me when he drew closer to the part of me that wanted touched the most. I cursed when he paused in his explorations.

Desperate for more, I rocked my ass against his hard-on with a pleading groan.

It was the best kind of torture as he kept his movements light and teasing. He traveled further south, tracing over the ridge of my hip, before moving down my leg. His touch moved up the inside of my thigh. The anticipation made me tremble, as everything in me begged for more. I couldn't hold in the needy noises as he ghosted over my balls, before running up my hard length.

When his hand retreated, I groaned, "Damn it, Luci. Stop teasing me!"

"But it's so much fun," he murmured in my ear in a deep, rumbling voice.

I rolled over to face him. Luci's playful expression disarmed my irritation, all of my complaints forgotten when he shifted positions to pin me down on the bed. His erection rested against me, hot and heavy, turning me on more. He stopped all my thoughts when he kissed me. It was a slow and tender exploration, further heightening my arousal.

He covered me in kisses, his lips and tongue continuing to tease me into a frenzy even while I luxuriated under the gentle worship. As much as I wanted to move on to the good stuff, I also enjoyed the gradual buildup to the bigger moment.

My patience didn't last long. Deciding to hell with subtlety, I reached for the nightstand where I'd left the lube before we had fallen asleep. I handed it to him, hoping he would get the hint. "I'm going to lose my damn mind if some part of you isn't inside me soon, Luci."

Instead of giving me instant relief, he took his time kissing down my body. The closer he got to my arousal, the harder it was for me to stay still. I bit my lip when his slicked fingers circled my entrance.

"Are you sure about this?"

"I've never been more certain about anything in my life." I spread my legs wider in silent invitation.

It was the permission Luci needed to proceed. He cautiously slid a lubed finger into me. It was sweet he didn't want to hurt me, but I had too much experience with anal to be coaxed into it.

"I can take more," I encouraged him.

He added a second finger, but it wasn't anywhere close to enough. Before I could demand more, he obliterated my words when he licked up the length of my member. *That* was unexpected—and welcomed. I got so lost in the moment it stunned me when he held my dick steady and hesitantly slid it into the wet warmth of his mouth.

That was more like it. I exclaimed, "Fuck, *yes*!"

It thrilled me when he inserted a third finger. As his confidence grew, he took me as far back into his throat as he could without gagging. It pushed me to my edge faster than I wanted.

"Shit, I'm so close, Luci," I whimpered, caressing his hair to help keep me grounded.

Rather than pulling off, he bobbed his head while massaging my sensitive bundle of nerves. I shouted his name as I came, unable to stop myself. He gagged but swallowed my release.

"Sorry, I—"

He interrupted me with an insistent kiss. The salty taste of myself in his mouth was an enormous turn-on for me. I couldn't believe he had gone down on me, let alone finished me. Some of my ex-girlfriends would spit afterward or forbid me from coming in their mouths, so for him to do that was astounding. I was breathless when I asked, "When the hell did you learn how to do that?"

His cheeks flushed. "Some of us can't sleep on planes."

"Are you telling me you researched all this stuff while I slept?" The revelation was too cute for words.

"There's only so many times you can refresh your inbox," he defended himself in embarrassment.

It was so quintessentially Luci that I laughed. That turned into a groan when he withdrew, leaving me almost unbearably empty. "Bless in-flight Wi-Fi. Maybe I should let you get bored more often." I loved his unrestrained laugh. "So, what else did you learn while I was dreaming about you?"

"Condoms?"

I was a big fan of instant gratification, but I couldn't resist the opportunity to push his buttons a little. That was one of my all-time favorite hobbies. "Wow, that's a little rudimentary, don't you think?"

He rolled his eyes. "No, smart-ass. I meant do you have any?"

Joking aside, I caressed his jaw as I told him, "I don't want anything between us. We're both clean, so—"

Luci breathed my name, before interrupting me to kiss me with a passion that stoked the flames of desire in me. When we paused for air, he slicked his hardness with lube and repositioned himself.

I had to remind myself to breathe as he entered me, going slow so as not to hurt me. The show of concern touched me, but I was too horny for the delicate-flower treatment. Instead, I hooked my legs behind his hips and forced him deeper into me. I arched up with pleasure, relishing his shocked gasp. I constricted my muscles around him, earning a flurry of broken swears.

"You're so fucking tight," he groaned, reflexively thrusting into me. "Shit, did I hurt you?"

"Do I sound like I'm hurting? I'm not fragile, Luci. Take me hard."

After that, there was no stopping us. It took him a few tries before he built up to a satisfying rhythm, but once he did, it was magical. All the dildos I had enjoyed over the years paled in comparison to his cock. The perfection of him filling me with his heat and delicious friction made me wonder how I'd ever go back to using unyielding silicone again. Then, I remembered that as long as he was my husband, I would never have to.

I clung to him, bracing my feet flat on the sheets for more traction as we moved together as one. Everything was right in my world as every roll of his hips sent me to new heights of ecstasy. I realized with startling clarity that I didn't need anything else if he was mine. I would be happy to spend the rest of my days basking in his whispered declarations of love, whole for the first time in my entire life.

Chapter 11

Luci

THERE WAS NO GREATER pleasure on Earth than being with Rhys. The sound of him calling out "Luci" with breathy moans was a beautiful symphony to my ears. Any reservations I had about changing my relationship with him had long disappeared. If this was what it meant to be his husband, I wouldn't have a single complaint. I wished I could drown in him and never come up for air again.

When I leaned forward to kiss him again, he cried out at the shift in angles. It was a noise of pure enjoyment. He had surrendered himself to me on every level, which was downright intoxicating.

The sight of him jerking off his renewed erection had me racing to my peak. My desire to be the only one responsible for his pleasure was at war with how hot it was to watch him touching himself. His noises grew desperate as he disrupted our rhythm from the overwhelming rush of sensations.

When I slowed down our pace, it earned me a cute growl of annoyance. I gripped his dick and started working it, refocusing him. "You're so fucking beautiful, and you're *mine*." My possessive declaration paired with a vigorous thrust rewarded me with a delicious keen. "Say it."

"I'm yours, Luci!" His gasps reached a fevered pitch, telling me he wouldn't be able to hold on for much longer. "I always have been."

Like I had in the honeymoon suite, I commanded, "Come for me, Rhys."

Two more strokes was all it took to send him over the edge. His cum splattered on my fist and his stomach as he shouted "Luci," his entire body shaking from the effort. It drew my orgasm as I growled his name, pushing all the way in as I climaxed. Only then did we still, both of us breathing heavily from the exertion.

Rhys tugged me down for a passionate kiss. He whispered "I love you," in between pecks, making my heart soar. It was a pure moment I would remember for the rest of my days.

He groaned when I withdrew to settle myself next to him, before sprawling out over my chest as we recovered our breath. I held him, never wanting to let go. There was no way I could ever return to being mere friends after knowing what it was like to be intimate with him.

I kissed his forehead and murmured, "I love you."

"That makes me the luckiest guy in the whole damn world." With effort, Rhys moved up to kiss me with such tenderness that I fell for him all over again. "I hope you understand I love you just as much."

"I might need another demonstration to be convinced."

He grinned. "You'll have to wait until after breakfast.

I'm too tired to get up and shower, let alone do anything else."

Unable to resist the temptation, I slid two of my fingers back into him. He pushed against me with a whimper, trying to take me deeper. "Something tells me I'll have no problem getting you up again."

His laugh got lost in a moan as I indulged in another taste of him.

Afterward, we ate a leisurely breakfast in the resort's outdoor restaurant overlooking the Aegean Sea. The view was breathtaking as the sunlight sparkled on the stunning blue water. I would happily stay in this gorgeous paradise for all of eternity with Rhys.

"It's beautiful here, isn't it?" he asked, looking out at the horizon.

"Yeah, it's so perfect it almost feels fake," I replied. The gentle breeze was refreshing. "I can't believe a place like this exists. Everything is so *blue*."

His gaze shifted over to me. "I'm so happy we're here together."

"I am, too." While true, my mind still boggled that we were here on our honeymoon. Would ever stop being surreal that he was my husband?

Rhys grinned as he added, "And I'm not just saying that because of all the sex we're going to have."

I chuckled at his response. "Good to know."

He turned serious. "I'm glad we'll have the chance to

spend some time together. When we were drinking in my hotel room, I realized how much I missed hanging out with you. I'm so sorry, Luci. I never should have let Olivia affect our friendship."

His sincere apology moved me. "I appreciate that."

Rhys reached out and took my left hand in his. "The only thing I regret more than wasting so many years with her is that I lost so much time with you." He brushed over my wedding ring, then caressed my knuckles. "What I did was unforgivable, but—"

I interrupted to assure him, "There's nothing to forgive."

His smile turned sad. "Maybe you've forgiven me already, but I haven't forgiven myself. I let Olivia come between us, which was the last thing in the world I wanted to happen."

"Don't beat yourself up over things you can't change," I told him. "All of that led us here. Being with you now matters more than what happened back then."

"Will you let me be with you now?"

I started to point out that he already was when I understood what he was really asking. Even though I was nervous by the unknown territory, my curiosity overrode it. I tugged him upright as I stood, taking advantage of the fact he was still holding my hand. "I'd like that very much."

"I'll make sure of it," Rhys promised in a tone that sent a shiver of anticipation through me.

Back in our room and stripped bare, Rhys set about learning every inch of my body. He took his time trailing kisses from my neck down as his fingertips tantalized me with the promise of what was to come.

He teased my nipple into a hard peak before continuing. "It's interesting that things are different now, yeah?"

"Hmm?"

He mirrored his actions on my other one, licking and sucking on it until it stiffened. "When we were teenagers, I was the more dominant one, but now I love when you get all authoritative with me."

"Is that your passive-aggressive way of suggesting I should overthrow you and take charge?"

"Don't you dare." He placed a kiss on each of my abs. "It's my turn."

"I was unaware this was turn-based."

He huffed in annoyance. "You know what I mean."

I did, but it was fun to play with him sometimes. "In my defense, I've gained more experience between then and now."

"It wasn't a criticism; it was merely an observation. I think it's unusual I'm the more assertive partner with women, but with you, I get so turned on by the thought of you dominating me. To be clear, that's not an invitation for right now. I'm talking about in general."

"Why does that surprise you?" I asked, amused when he licked along the ridge of my hip. He certainly was being thorough. "You've always relied on me because you trust that I'll help you through your anxiety or anything bad that happens. It's probably an extension of that dynamic."

He paused in his explorations as he considered my words. "Huh, I guess I like you having control over me on a deeper level than I realized—just not this second. Later is good, though."

I snorted at that. "You keep saying that like I've threatened to stop you. I haven't moved since you started taking your sweet-ass time exploring."

"Yes, because you have the patience of the saint you were named after." He kissed the mole above my hip. I had no idea why he liked that so much, but the enjoyment he derived from it entertained me. "I've waited too long for this chance, so I refuse to rush, thank you very much."

I reached down and caressed his cheek to get his attention. "This isn't a onetime offer, Rhys."

There was a shadow of doubt in his eyes. "But what if you don't like it?"

To soothe him, I kept my tone playful. "You might not have heard of it, but there's this thing called the internet that you can use to research anything. It's a fantastic resource for this kind of stuff. I've had great success with it, as you will recall."

"Yeah, but if you hate it—"

I cut him off. "Then we'll do some homework on how to make it better for the next time, that's all. Stop putting that pressure on yourself. I won't permanently ban you from my ass if this is something less than the apex of sexual nirvana, okay?" He laughed, but some of his concerns lingered. "What's really bothering you?"

Rhys squirmed before he admitted, "I didn't like it my first time trying anal, so I'm worried you won't, either."

"What didn't you like about it?"

He trailed his fingers over the rigid length of my erection, which welcomed the touch. "I was impatient and rushed, so it hurt like hell. I had no clue what I was doing."

"But you tried it again, then discovered you liked it. Why would you assume I wouldn't be the same in that situation?"

"I just want your first real time to be as good for you as it was for me," he said in a small voice.

My ego purred at hearing he enjoyed himself, but I focused on the bigger issue. "You learned your lesson not to go too fast, so we'll be fine. Stop worrying, or I'll flip you over and figure out how to bottom from the top."

"The phrase is 'top from the bottom,' actually. Although, I totally proved your point about taking control in the face of my anxiety, didn't it?"

"I'll refrain from doing a victory dance if you hurry up and get on with it."

Rhys kissed me lovingly, then renewed his exploration by pressing his lips against my chin, then down my neck.

I grumbled over the setback. "Is there some reason you're testing the limits of my patience?" His amused snicker told me he knew exactly what he was doing. "Do you want me to beg?"

"You could try it."

My desperation for something more substantial made it less embarrassing to arch my back and wantonly plead, "Please, stop teasing me, Rhys. I need you inside me, so *please*."

The blazing desire returned to his burning gaze. "Oh, I think I enjoy having you at my mercy."

"Then do something about it, damn it!"

Despite my earlier confidence, the lube cap flipping open set off a flutter of nervousness through me. While Rhys had obviously enjoyed himself as I pleasured him, there was a part of me that feared it would be painful. He distracted me by licking down the seam of my balls, before sensuously kissing one of them. When he sucked on it, I gasped as he proved I wasn't the only person who had done his research.

Rhys pressed a slicked finger into me, but I barely noticed as he switched to my other ball. He lavished it with attention before checking in with me. "You're good?"

"I'll be better when you use more than one finger."

He carefully inserted a second into me. I felt the stretch of it, but his slow pace kept it from hurting. It went a long way toward easing my apprehensions. Once again, he refocused my attention when he began teasing my dick with his tongue, sucking only the tip in a prelude to what I was after.

"Of course you're a goddamn cocktease," I groaned. It

was in line with his personality, but it drove me crazy with a need for more. His knowing laughter made me bang my head on the pillow in frustration. "Haven't you tried my patience enough today?"

He delighted in reminding me, "You're the one who said I shouldn't go fast."

"I take it back. This is torture."

"Yes, but it's the fun kind." He interrupted my next complaint by gingerly attempting to add a third finger. The initial burn of it caused me to inhale sharply, but him stopping was way worse.

"I'm fine," I assured him, preferring not to backtrack.

Rhys stubbornly insisted, "No, I won't hurt you." To avoid antagonizing his anxiety, I bit back my complaints as he continued stretching me. The process was tedious, but when he inserted another one again, it lacked the previous discomfort.

Satisfied I wasn't in pain, he returned to his blow job as he diligently prepared me. He gained more confidence, taking me in deeper as he worked me from the inside. When he applied the right amount of pressure to my prostate, I came without warning from the unexpected burst of pleasure.

"Sorry, I—"

He wiped the corner of his mouth with the back of his hand. "Why are you apologizing—because I did a great job?"

"You've got me on that one."

Rhys spread his fingers to test how I was doing. "How does this feel?"

"Like we can move on."

"Ooh, nice answer." He withdrew and put on a show of coating his prick with lube. "I'll go slow, okay?"

"How could you go any slower? This pace is positively glacial."

He ignored my smart-ass comment as he positioned himself to penetrate me. It was more awkward than painful as he cautiously pushed into me. I reminded myself to relax and not be impatient as I adjusted to accommodate his girth. It felt like forever before he slid in all the way.

His voice was tight with restraint as he asked, "Does it hurt?"

I resisted the urge to make another smart-aleck remark, aware that his concern stemmed from his anxiety. "No, it's just...odd."

"Odd is better than ow. Can I move yet? Or do you need more time—"

"Yes, please move," I requested, more than ready for the strange fullness to morph into something better.

Rhys began with a gentle roll of his hips, building up to more deliberate movements. It frustrated me when it did nothing for me. I hooked a leg over him in an attempt at shifting to a different position. It was a slight improvement, but it was far from satisfying.

I swore when he stilled. "Goddamn it, don't stop. I promise, you're not hurting me at all."

"I'm also not making you feel good, but I have an idea." He guided my long legs over his shoulders, then shifted closer to bring my hips up more. For a brief second, I was self-conscious about the position, but that changed when he resumed.

There was an instant difference as he struck deeper, causing my toes to curl with bliss. "Oh, that's *much* better," I gasped, grasping at the sheets as I moaned. "*So* much better, fuck!"

"You'll feel even more incredible soon." He ran his hands up my thighs before grabbing my ass and using it to pull me closer with every thrust. That had me shouting at how fantastic it was.

"Harder!"

It gratified me when Rhys obeyed without questioning if I could handle it. I never imagined his balls hitting against me as he fucked me would be so arousing, but damned if it didn't do it for me. As I grew louder, he started pounding into me until I was almost bent in half. It was an all-consuming pleasure that left no place for any thoughts.

I hadn't even noticed when I began getting hard again, but I roughly tugged on my cock as I raced toward my climax. When Rhys came in me, it sent me over the edge. My whole body arched from the intensity of my release.

When he pulled out of me, I felt weirdly empty. I remembered to lower my legs from his shoulders, which allowed him to collapse on my chest, a position that was becoming his favorite.

I wrapped my arms around him, still dazed from the experience. He absentmindedly stroked the small mole on my neck. If I had had the energy to laugh, I would have. As far as quirks went, it was one of his cuter ones. It made me feel good to know he loved all of me, down to every one of my beauty marks.

We remained in companionable silence for a while, before Rhys joked, "I'd ask how I did, but I'm pretty sure I know the answer to that question."

"See? You worried for nothing." I ruffled his hair. "*Wow*."

"Wow is right," he agreed with a tired chuckle. "If it's this amazing our first time, I can't even fathom how incredible it'll be ten years from now."

My heart swelled with love for him, hearing him speaking about us in the long-term. "I look forward to finding out." He made a happy noise as he snuggled closer. We lazed together, in no rush to do anything other than be with each other.

Chapter 12

Rhys

THE FIRST WEEK OF our honeymoon had been the best of my entire life. Luci worshipped me with utter love and devotion. While I preferred bottoming, the few times I had topped had been incredible. Sex with him was the most satisfying I had ever had, but there was one need of mine we hadn't explored yet.

After our swim in our private villa's infinity pool overlooking the ocean, he observed me while I kept my distance in the shower. I deflected his attempts to start something, hoping to provoke his urge to dominate me. When we pretended to have sex to piss off Olivia, the glimpse of his sexy authority was tantalizing. I ached for a taste of it. Instead of driving him to action, he grew concerned. While sweet, it also made me want to scream with frustration.

When I rejected another advance and got out of the shower, Luci followed me. "Have I done something wrong?"

I shook my head as I dried off with a towel. My desire to tell him what I was after warred with my need for him to manhandle me without having to ask for it. It had never appealed to me before, but it was all I could think about now. We had talked about how much I liked him being in control, but his need to cherish me kept him from giving me the aggressive roughness I was after.

"Please talk to me, Rhys."

His expression of genuine worry made me feel bad, but I was too horny to stop being a brat. I tilted my chin with a defiant look. "No."

Luci narrowed his blue eyes, sending a thrill through me. This time, his request came out as a demand. "Tell me."

I appealed to his competitive side by challenging, "Make me."

When he continued looking down at me with a puzzled expression, I turned on my heel and walked into the bedroom. I assumed he would follow me to find out why I was acting this way. What I didn't expect was him throwing my back up against the wall and pinning me in place with his larger body.

There was a dark fire in his eyes as he growled, "Wrong answer."

I was erect in an instant, my soul ignited by the spark of lust his action inspired. I pressed my hardness against him so he would understand his dominance was what I was after. "What are you going to do about it?"

His reply came in the form of a savage kiss. There was no finesse in it as our tongues clashed in battle with an angry hunger fueling us. I strained against his hold on both of my pinned wrists, but he tightened his grasp and pushed back harder. I moaned in ecstasy as he gave me a taste of what I wanted.

We both panted when we broke apart. I remained defiant, albeit breathy as I taunted, "You'll never get an answer out of me if that's the best you can do."

He released a wrist to grab my erection, getting my full attention. "You're already dripping for me." He rubbed the bead of precum that had gathered. His gruff voice got me all hot and bothered. "Do you think I can't get what I want from you?"

"You'll have to take it by force," I snarled. I wanted him to fuck me so hard I couldn't move for hours afterward.

"I can do that."

That was the only warning I received before he threw me over his shoulder, causing my breath to whoosh out of me from the suddenness of it. He didn't give me any time to recover before he roughly tossed me onto the bed. When I sat up, he shoved me down and pinned me by the neck. His show of strength aroused me even further.

He pressed the full weight of his body against me, letting me feel how hard he was. "Maybe I should teach you a lesson you'll never forget."

"What lesson?"

"What happens when you defy me." Before I responded, he crushed his lips against mine again.

It was exhilarating, but I still pushed his buttons. The payoff would be worth it. "Is that all you've got?"

"You *will* give in to me." The unspoken *or else* made

me tremble at the promise. I wanted to, but I needed dominated in the process to get the satisfaction I was after.

"Never!"

I couldn't believe how fast he flipped me onto my stomach with my ass up in the air. He ran his fingers down my crack to spread my cheeks, revealing my hole. I bit back a whimper as he toyed with me by hinting at penetration.

His arrogant laugh as he teased me was so damn sexy. He made an exaggerated *pop* sound as he removed his finger from his mouth to press the wet tip of it into me. "This part of you seems eager to give me what I want." He withdrew it when I said nothing.

"I—"

That was as far as I made it before I yelped at the unfamiliar sensation of his tongue running over my entrance.

He chuckled at my reaction. "That seemed to shut you up."

"You wish," I spat, despite being more turned on than I had ever been before.

His hand came forward, stroking my erection. "It's obvious you want to give in to me. Why continue this pointless resistance?"

It spurred me to take a risk. "Fuck you!"

"Actually, I'll be the one fucking you tonight, sweetheart," he purred, making me quiver with desire. He had never used a pet name for me before, but I *really* liked it.

His tongue circled over my hole again, before he

spread me open to dip it in further. He didn't pause as he rimmed me like a pro. It was unlike anything I had experienced before. When he added his fingers into the mix, I dropped my head to rest on my forearms with a whimper, trembling from overwhelming desire.

"Where's your defiance now?"

It took an effort to snarl, "Go fuck yourself!"

I shouted in surprise when he nipped at my ass. "Wrong answer again, sweetheart." It was beyond me why that was so sexy.

Luci always carefully prepared me to receive him, so it was a total shock when the head of his slicked erection entered me already. "Will you be obedient, or do I need to show you who's the one really in control here?"

I grinned to myself as I shoved back hard, forcing him in to the hilt. The resulting fullness caused me to shout with satisfaction.

He threaded his fingers through my hair, then used the grip to jerk my head up to murmur in my ear, "That was unwise."

"Don't care. Fuck me!" I may have wanted dominated, but that wouldn't stop me from being bossy to antagonize him.

His hand moved to the front of my throat, caressing the side before tightening to where I had to gasp for air. His voice was dark and sexy as he reminded me, "You're not the one in control right now. I am."

He forced me forward, pinning me facedown on the bed by the back of my neck. Instead of the slow love-making I had been enjoying our whole honeymoon, Luci fucked me hard and fast, pounding me into the mattress.

It was everything I wanted and then some. I cried out with abandon, rubbing against the sheets for relief. At this rate, I wouldn't last long.

Once he realized what I was doing, Luci grasped my dick, squeezing it tight enough to make me gasp. "No, only I can give you pleasure."

I tried thrusting into his fist, but he released me, causing me to whine low in my throat over being denied.

He taunted, "What was that? Did you say you're ready to submit to me?"

My shaky "no" wouldn't convince anybody, let alone him.

He laughed as he continued taking me aggressively. "What was that? I didn't quite hear you."

I stayed silent, although it took a supreme effort. It was difficult to contain my excitement over Luci playing this game with me.

Once again, he used my hair to yank me backward to his chest. "I won't be satisfied until you're screaming my name. Let me hear you, sweetheart."

I didn't understand why the taunting nickname did it for me, but it was hot as fuck. It was a good thing we didn't have neighbors near our private villa, because I shouted his name until my voice cracked. He mercilessly wrung every whimper and moan out of me with his harsh pleasure. I loved every second.

It surprised both of us when he triggered my climax

by tugging on the shell of my ear with his teeth. That was something we would have to explore later.

"Did I give you permission to come?"

"I'm sorry," I gasped, my body still moving in time with his despite my release.

Luci abruptly stopped. "Now, I really will have to punish you."

When he pulled out of me, I groaned from the loss. Before I could plead for respite, I was flat on my back in the wet spot. He looked down at me with smug superiority, before his expression softened.

He lifted my hips and slid in slow. All trace of roughness disappeared as he began tenderly making love to me, taking his time demolishing what little composure I had. Even though I was spent, he encouraged me back to hardness with his gentle teasing.

"Now do you believe me that your heart, body, mind, and soul all belong to me?"

I almost sobbed when he took my renewed erection in hand and worked it. The overload of pleasure left me raw. It pressed me to my limits as he kept me on the cusp of climax. Whenever I got close, he backed off again. Desperate for relief, the word "Please" escaped me from me.

"Please what?"

If he thought I could form a complete sentence, he was sorely mistaken. I begged with more urgency, "*Please!*"

In response, Luci withdrew until only the tip remained.

I made an anguished noise, trying and failing to force him deeper.

His tone was gentle but still commanding as he asked, "What do you want, sweetheart?" This time he said the pet name like a verbal caress that reduced me to a puddle.

"You." I wanted that more than anything else.

He slid in with agonizing slowness until he was balls-deep in me again. "Do you give in to me?"

There was no resistance left in me. "Yes!"

He kissed me again, sucking on my bottom lip. After a few gentle rolls of his hips, he came inside me with a soft moan.

A single touch from him induced my second climax. I almost passed out from the intensity of my release, leaving me trembling in the wake. As much as I wished I could thank him for giving me what I wanted and then some, I was beyond words. I slipped into sleep with a smile on my face as he cradled me against his strong chest.

Chapter 13

Luci

AFTER A WEEK OF living in paradise with Rhys, I was ready to renounce my old life in Sunnyside and permanently move to Greece with him. After so many years of being in denial, being allowed to love him openly was an incredible gift. It almost seemed too good to be true, but I ignored my inner pessimist who expected everything to fall apart like it always did. I would hold on to this happiness for as long as I could.

As I dealt with my overflowing work emails, I resented reality for encroaching on our time together. Since I hadn't planned for our impromptu elopement and honeymoon, I hadn't prepared to take off two weeks without warning. My selfish actions had thrown my entire company into chaos, but they were doing an admirable job of scrambling to cover my unexpected absence. The least I could do was stay on top of my inbox.

I welcomed Rhys's touch as he massaged my shoulders. He suggested, "Come on, let's get lunch."

It was hard to not give in to what we both wanted,

but I stoically said, "You can go ahead. I'll catch up soon. I just need to finish a few more things first."

"Fine, I'll order one of those delicious drinks I can't pronounce while I wait." Rhys gave me a sweet, lingering kiss which I savored. "Don't keep me waiting too long. You know how I get when I'm hangry."

I chuckled, well aware of how he turned into a petulant brat whenever he got too hungry. It was as true now as when we were kids. "I'll do my best."

"You always do." He kissed the top of my head, then left for the outdoor cabana.

Once I reached a stopping point, I hurried to meet Rhys at the restaurant. I caught sight of him at the bar talking with someone, but it wasn't until I came closer that I recognized his ex-girlfriend, Miranda. Out of all of his past girlfriends, she was the only one I had ever approved of. Her laid-back attitude and complete disinterest in Rhys's family had made her a great match for him, but their fierce stubbornness had led to their breakup. She was still gorgeous in her bikini that barely contained her ample breasts. With her elegant features and stunning figure, she looked like a goddess on vacation in paradise.

I started to approach with an apology when Miranda scolded him, "Seriously, what the hell were you thinking, Rhys? Marriage? *You?*" Her words stopped me dead in my tracks, hidden behind a pillar where I could spy on them.

"I know, I know." He ran his fingers through his dark

blond hair with a heavy sigh. "In my defense, it *seemed* like a good idea."

She asked with a scornful laugh, "Since when has marriage been the answer to anything?"

"I didn't have any other choice," he insisted. "I went along with it, thinking it wouldn't be *that* bad. But it was a disaster in the making."

"On the scale of all the dumbass decisions you've made, this definitely ranks high on your list."

Rhys took a sip of his drink before saying, "It's safe to say it's the worst decision I've made in my life. I regret ever letting things get that far."

His words were a punch in the stomach. It forced me to question whether anything this past week had been real. I had never been so happy, but apparently it was all built on a lie.

"Your stubborn streak gets you into trouble every time." Miranda laughed. "I know that better than anyone."

He smiled sadly. "If I had the chance to do it all over again, I would never agree to marriage. I don't know why I thought it would be the answer to all of my problems. It's not like it was about love."

Tears sprung to my eyes at hearing he regretted our marriage and wished he could undo it. But the worst pain was he didn't love me. Why would he lie to me?

I barely heard Miranda tell him, "I'm pretty sure you *weren't* thinking. That's the real problem."

"No, the bigger problem is the mess I have to clean up once I get back stateside." He grimaced. "It's easy to pretend everything is fine when I'm here. But it's going to turn into an ugly shitshow once I'm home and have to deal with the consequences of all this."

"Well, that's what happens when you make shitty impulse decisions," she teased. "Good luck."

"I'll definitely need it."

When they both laughed, I couldn't take it anymore. I fled to our room and started packing my things. I refused to stay and act like everything was okay. Not when marrying me was Rhys's biggest regret. He had ripped my heart out of my chest and stomped on it, shattering my beautiful illusion he was as happy as I was with our marriage. It destroyed me to discover the genuine love I thought we shared as we intimately connected on the deepest level was nothing but a lie. I didn't want to accept the fact Rhys had stubbornly committed to enduring his bad decision until we returned to Sunnyside and he could annul our union. But I'd heard him loud and clear.

I cried as I booked my plane ticket home on the next flight. It was the coward's way out, but hearing him tell someone else how much he regretted marrying me was more than I could endure. I wouldn't survive him telling me the truth to my face—or even worse, lying to me that we were happy together.

The pain of forcing my wedding band off my finger paled in comparison to my devastation over this discovery. I was the biggest idiot in the world to believe Rhys loved me. When had I ever been that lucky?

I placed the diamond ring on top of the signed annulment paperwork I'd printed out in Vegas before he told me he wanted to make our marriage work. The foolish part of me wished I could rip it up and pretend I hadn't overheard how miserable he was with our decision. If I did, we could continue pretending to be happy. But it was impossible when it was all a lie. I loved him enough to do the mature thing and let him go, even though it broke me into a million little pieces.

As I left our honeymoon villa to head to the airport, it felt like nothing would ever be okay again. I had never lived without Rhys at my side, but I would have to learn. Maybe one day it wouldn't hurt anymore. But that day wasn't today.

Chapter 14

Rhys

When Luci hadn't come to meet me for lunch, it had worried me. When I got to the room and found his wedding ring and signed annulment papers on the bed, that worry turned to full-blown panic. I didn't understand what had changed in that short time between when I'd kissed him goodbye and when I came back to find him gone. The concierge confirmed that Luci took the shuttle to the airport, so I started packing my things while my personal assistant, Xander, remotely booked my trip home. Unfortunately, luck was not on my side. The flight he was on had already sold out, so the earliest I could leave would be first thing the next morning.

With Luci there, our honeymoon villa had felt like paradise. Without him, it was a purgatory of the worst kind. As I sat there miserable and alone, I wracked my brain trying to understand where everything went wrong. Eventually, it occurred to me that maybe he'd come to the cabana and saw me chatting with Miranda. Did he see me with her and think I wanted to be with her or another woman again?

After twenty agonizing hours on my delayed flight to

Sunnyside, I was no closer to an answer about what had caused him to leave me. However, I would do anything to get him back. Even the one day we had spent apart was too much. I made a quick stop after landing to pick something up before I went straight to Luci's house. I refused to spend a single second away from him if I didn't have to.

I rang his doorbell repeatedly, to no avail. It had a camera that alerted on his phone who was there, so I pleaded, "Please let me in, Luci. We need to talk."

There was a prolonged silence, making me think he wasn't home. But his voice came through the speaker. "Leave, Rhys. There's nothing to say."

"Maybe you don't have anything to say, but I have plenty."

"There's no point. You have what you need. Go."

"Either you let me in, or I'm using my key and coming in," I warned. "One way or the other, we are having this conversation, even if I have to broadcast it to all of your neighbors by having it through your damn doorbell. I know you don't want that."

Once again, the silence dragged out between us. I started fishing for my keys in my pocket when the front door opened, revealing Luci. He was wearing black sweats and an emerald-green T-shirt, which showed off his well-defined arm muscles. As delicious as that was, it concerned me because he looked like he hadn't slept once since leaving Greece. I tried to hug him, but he stepped out of the way to avoid me. The rejection stung, but I would do whatever it took to make things better.

I walked into Luci's living room and sat on his couch. He kept his distance, but I rejected the brush-off. I moved closer to sit next to him.

Luci shifted uncomfortably as he stared down at me with so much sadness I almost forgot how to breathe. "What are you doing here?"

"Getting answers about why you disappeared without saying goodbye."

"It was better for you if I wasn't there, so I left."

That hadn't been the answer I expected. "Why would you think that?"

He silently started down at his hands as his thumb rubbed over the spot where his wedding band had been. His skin showed a slight indent from the ring, and a faint tan line from our time in our villa's infinity pool.

"Is this because you saw me with Miranda?"

Once again, he said nothing as he continued avoiding my gaze. He was bigger than me, but he seemed almost impossibly small on the couch, as if he had deflated in his grief.

"Please tell me you didn't leave because you assumed I'd rather be with her instead of you." I would kill him if that was why he left.

That earned me a slight frown. "No, that thought hadn't crossed my mind."

"Then, why the hell would you leave me?" I asked, my voice cracking in my despair.

Luci took a deep breath before saying, "You said you regretted our marriage as the worst decision of your life, so—"

His words made me realize he had overheard my conversation with Miranda but misunderstood the most important part of it. I interrupted him, using his full name, so he knew how serious I was. "Lucien, I wasn't talking about *our* marriage when I said it was the worst decision of my life that I regret. I was talking about my impending marriage with *Olivia*."

Luci's eyebrows furrowed in confusion. "But you said you regretted letting things get that far. You told her if you had the chance to do it all over again, you would never agree to marriage because it wasn't about love."

"Yes, I regretted staying in my relationship with Olivia and letting things get to the point of almost walking down the aisle. If I had the chance to change everything, I never would have dated her, let alone agreed to marry her. I never loved her. How could I when I love you?"

He looked scared to believe me. "But what about dealing with the consequences when you came home?"

"Olivia was trying to sell my house. Xander changed my locks to keep her out, but there's stuff with the Realtor that only I can take care of. She has all of her shit at my place that she needs to pick up. I also have things at her apartment, but I'm sure she's burned everything by now. At some point, I have to deal with my parents whenever they decide they want to talk to me again. Those were the consequences I meant, Luci."

"But I thought..."

When he trailed off, I reached out and took his face in my hands, forcing him to hold my gaze. "Yes, our marriage was an impulse decision, but I don't regret it for a second. Out of all my many, many bad ideas, marrying you was the best thing I've ever done. I love you, Luci. Even when you do stupid shit like sacrificing yourself because you think that will somehow make me happy." He chuckled at that. "But what could ever make me happier than being with you?"

I leaned forward and brushed my lips against his. When he didn't pull away, I kissed him with all my love for him. As he wrapped his arms around me to hold me closer, I knew that everything would be okay between us.

Even though I could kiss him forever, I stopped. The flash of uncertainty in Luci's expressive blue eyes pained me, but I knew what I was about to do would help. I pulled a ring box out of my pocket and got onto one knee on the floor. "You've been my entire world since we were kids. I'm sorry I was too stupid to understand back then I loved you, but I love you more than life itself now. Will you still be my husband?"

I opened the blue velvet box, revealing the engagement ring I'd picked up on my way over from the airport. While we were in Greece, I had arranged with Cathy at the jewelry store to have it custom made. I wanted him to have his own ring and not just Olivia's. The platinum band held a solitaire in the center of the tension setting. On either side of it were alternating round brilliants and baguette diamonds that matched the design of his original one.

He asked in disbelief, "You want to stay married to me?"

"Not only do I want to stay married, I want to have a proper wedding so that our family and all of our friends can come. I want everyone to see how happy and in love we are."

"I want that, too." He leaned down to kiss me, sending my heart soaring with joy. "Yes, I'll marry you again, Rhys."

With a trembling hand, I slid the engagement ring on his finger. I was pleased it fit perfectly this time. Unable to resist, I teased, "Good, because I already invited Cathy since she helped me with the rings. She was *very* excited to find out I married the right person."

Luci's laughter healed the hurt of him leaving. "Wait, rings?" His gaze dropped to my hand, which was missing my wedding band.

"We deserve matching bands. Cathy is having new custom ones made for us," I explained. "Before she gets started, she wants you to come in and sign off on the design, though. I didn't want to make all the decisions without your input."

He grinned, chasing away all the dark clouds in his eyes. "Great, now I can apologize in person for laughing so hard at her thinking we were the ones getting married."

"Something tells me she'll get a kick out of that." I stood up, holding my hand out to him. "Let me show you how much I love you, Luci."

We walked with our fingers interlaced into his bedroom. As I stripped him bare, it thrilled me to know that he was mine forever.

I wasted no time in casting off my own clothes so I could pin him down on his bed. With great pleasure, I showed him with my lips, tongue, and fingertips how much I wanted him. I didn't want there to be a single doubt in his mind about how much I loved and adored him.

It was a heady feeling having him surrender himself to me. The love and trust he had in me made my heart swell with pride. I intended to treasure him for the rest of my days.

Once I finished preparing him, I slid my slicked cock into him. I built up to a steady rhythm, telling him with my body and words how much I cherished him. His moans of satisfaction sent my desire spiraling higher. Nothing was more beautiful than the sight of him arching up and sighing under me as I pleasured him. It was the best feeling in the world knowing every day of the rest of our lives would be like this.

After almost forty-eight hours of a very stressful period without sleep, I couldn't hold out as long as I wanted to. I came after he did, overwhelmed by my emotions for the incredible man who had been by my side for my entire life. "Luci, I love you so much."

"I love you, too." He moaned as we kissed, his body still intimately embracing me. There was nowhere else I would rather be than right there with him forever.

Epilogue

Luci

ONE YEAR LATER

Since waking up married to Rhys in Las Vegas, life had never been better. To celebrate our one-year anniversary, we held a "proper" wedding for everyone to be there when we renewed our vows. The ceremony had been beautiful. Now, in front of all our family and friends, we had our first dance together at our reception to Jason Mraz and Colbie Caillat's "Lucky."

"You know, I still think we should have had Elvis's 'Burning Love' be our first dance."

I chuckled at the memory of him walking down the aisle to that song when we eloped. "That's not something you slow dance to."

"As you will recall, I also suggested that we could wow everyone with our sexy Argentine tango, but *somebody* said no."

"Trust me, nobody wants to watch us doing the ballroom equivalent of sex on the dance floor."

He sighed in mock defeat. "It's probably for the best. Your sister would have scored us an eight just to piss me off." Rhys and Lucretia had a longstanding habit of competitively watching celebrity ballroom dancing shows together. Most amusingly, they commented on everything as if they were the foremost experts, despite never having taken a single dance lesson in their lives. "We totally would deserve a ten."

"I'm sure she would cut us some slack since it's our wedding day."

Rhys arched an eyebrow at me as he sarcastically asked, "I'm sorry, have you met Lucretia? At her most generous, she's stricter than any judge."

"And you're different how?" They both took their reality shows way too seriously, which was as true now as it had been when we were teenagers. I loved listening to their snarky digs.

"Fair enough." He grinned. "Do you know what's my favorite part of having an official wedding?"

I couldn't resist teasing him a little. "We get cake this time?"

"Okay, besides the cake."

"Our family is here for it?" Much to our surprise, Rhys's mother had helped persuade his father to come around to our marriage. The fact that his family was here —and happy for us—was huge.

He leaned closer, his breath tickling my ear as he murmured, "We get a second honeymoon. Three full weeks of sex and sunshine with the love of my life." Rhys had been most insistent on a three-week honeymoon; two weeks for a "normal" one, and an extra week to make up for the one we lost when I left him in Greece last year.

"When we reach the Maldives Luxurian Suites Resort, I'm going to—"

The spark of lust that burned bright in Rhys's eyes set my whole soul on fire. It took incredible willpower not to ravage his mouth and drown in the taste and feel of him. I interrupted him. "Stop that thought right there. I have no desire to get a hard-on in front of the almost three hundred people staring at us."

His grin turned impish. "For all you know, I could have finished that sentence by saying, 'I'm going to pass out face-first on the bed and sleep forever after the insanely long flight there.'"

"I know you better than that."

"Yeah, you do." He smiled at me with so much affection that it stole my breath away. "I love you, Luci."

He snuggled against me, making me smile when he reflexively kissed the small mole on my neck, then laid his head on my shoulder as we continued moving to the music. I rested my chin on top of him, loving how he fit against me. He was my missing puzzle piece that had finally made me whole. "I love you just as much, sweetheart."

"Eloping was the best bad idea ever, huh?"

"Only you could turn a terrible idea into a happy ever after."

He laughed. "Does that make you my Prince Charming?"

"It makes me your loving and devoted husband forever."

Rhys's smile was beautiful as he gazed at me like I was his entire world. "That's even better."

We kissed to loud cheers. As the song said, I was lucky to be in love with my best friend. More than that, I was blessed to be married to him.

Thank you for reading **Bet on Love**! Want to see more of Luci and Rhys? A bonus chapter about their house hunting adventure with a visual guide is available to my newsletter subscribers. To read it, visit my website at www.ariellazoelle.com to sign up!

Next up is **Love Means More**! You definitely won't want to miss Ambrose and Augie's funny and steamy romance. If you love best friends to lovers, fake boyfriends, and bisexual awakening romances, you'll adore their story.

Thank You

THANK YOU FOR READING *Bet on Love*. I love hearing from readers, so please consider leaving a review and letting everyone know how much you enjoyed it.

Reviews are crucial for helping new readers discover me and decide whether or not they want to take a chance on my books. If you could take a moment to share your thoughts, I'd really appreciate it!

Recommending my work to others is also a huge help, so if you liked this book, please consider spreading the word to others!

About the Series

THANK YOU TO EVERYONE for going on this little detour with me. It was really fun to do something new and I hope you enjoyed the cuteness of Luci and Rhys. If you want to see their house hunting adventures, don't forget to sign up for my newsletter to read their extra epilogue.

This **Good Bad Idea** series is seven books long and features characters that are interconnected. However, the books can still be read in any order. That means this isn't the last we'll see Luci and Rhys!

Love Means More is the second book in the series. It features Rhys's groomsmen from Chapter 8, Ambrose O'Rourke and August Murphy. Their story begins immediately after the conclusion of that chapter when they leave Luci and Rhys's honeymoon suite. It's a hilarious friends to lovers, fake boyfriends, bisexual awakening romance. If you like playful banter and sexy fun, definitely check it out! Luci and Rhys also appear in it, so you won't want to miss it.

Rhys's personal assistant, Xander Dandridge, who also appeared in Chapter 8, is the focus of the fourth book in the series, **Love Fool**. It's a friends to lovers, fake boyfriends, opposites attract romance with his best friend, Jules Tourneau. If you love hilarious and sexy books, this is another one you should check out!

Next in Series

Can fake dating his best friend lead to real romance for Ambrose and Augie?

AMBROSE O'ROURKE

I've dropped at least 1,846,957 hints that I want to be more than Augie's best friend. Despite my best efforts, my reputation as a straight playboy means he's not picking up what I'm putting down. If I'm going to win his heart, I've got to get creative.

Maybe if I show him what an awesome fake boyfriend I am, he'll want me to be his real one?

AUGUST "AUGIE" MURPHY

Secretly being in love with your straight friend sucks. Secretly being in love with your straight friend who won't quit flirting with you *really* sucks. When Ambrose suggests we go on a fake double date as boyfriends, the temptation is too much to resist. Even if we're only pretending for one night, I want to know what it's like to be loved by him.

Is it possible to turn my fake boyfriend for a night into my real one forever?

Love Means More is the second book in the *Good Bad Idea* series and part of the Sunnyside universe. This novel features a friends to lovers, fake boyfriends, bisexual awakening romance. Full of cute sweetness and sexy fun, every story ends with a satisfying HEA and no cliffhangers. Each book can be read as a standalone or as part of the series in order.

Also by Ariella Zoelle

For a complete and up-to-date list of Ariella Zoelle's releases, please visit her website at

www.ariellazoelle.com

GOOD BAD IDEA SERIES

Bet on Love

Love Means More

Fancy Love

Love Fool

Love Directions

Picture Love

Love Practice

STANDALONES

Battle for the Top

SUITE DREAMS SERIES

Snowbody Like You

Flawsome Explorations

Acknowledgements

I can't thank my friends enough for putting up with my insane schedule of late. It's been a challenge trying to balance all of my responsibilities, so I'm very grateful for everyone being understanding that my life has not been my own for quite some time now.

An extra special thank you goes out to all of my readers who have been willing to go on this light-hearted novella adventure with me. It's been a fun change of pace, as well as the most fun writing I've had in a while.

This *Good Bad Idea* series started on a whim in January, so I'm eternally thankful that Pam and Sandra were kind enough to accommodate my schedule on such short notice in making this book happen so fast. It's been very exciting working with them, and I really appreciate how they helped polish this into something amazing.

This may end up being a year of great change, but I will continue to do my best to keep writing at the forefront of my priorities. Thank you to everyone for being part of my journey. I can't wait to meet again in **Love Means More**.

About the Author

WWW.ARIELLAZOELLE.COM

Ariella Zoelle previously published as A.F. Zoelle. She adores steamy, funny, swoony romances where couples are allowed to just be happy. That means she writes low angst stories full of heat, humor, and heart. Her vast knowledge of weird, wild, and wonderful randomness colors her writing, meaning her characters have some pretty strange and entertaining interests.

There are even rumors that she's a time management wizard who uses her magic powers to create enough free time to turn her massive horde of plot bunnies into sassy M/M romance novels. Her next feat will be turning herself into a full-time author.

For more information on new releases and access to exclusive content, sign up for Ariella Zoelle's newsletter. To subscribe, visit her website at www.ariellazoelle.com.

You can also join her Facebook Group, Ariella Zoelle's Sunnyside, at www.facebook.com/groups/amazingafzoelle, or follow her on Twitter and Instagram at @ariellazoelle.

Made in the USA
Monee, IL
24 June 2021